UNDYING LOVE

J.M. GOODRICH

UNDYING LOVE

J.M. GOODRICH

Undying Love

Copyright 2022 J.M. Goodrich

Cover by Averi Hope, Averi Hope Designs

Edited by Natalie Guillaumier Owens

Formatted by Jennifer Laslie

Honoria

I parked my beat-up old Toyota in my parent's driveway, turning off the ignition. It was eerie, seeing every light turned off. The house looked cold, empty, devoid of life. Usually, there would be some type of movement going on inside, some sign of life. Now, there was none. Nothing. An empty void where a happy, loving family once dwelled. Staring at their house, my throat grew dry as tears pricked at the back of my eyes.

I sat here, in the seat of my car, for what seemed like hours. Stepping foot inside that house would make everything seem that much more real. And I wasn't quite ready to face that reality yet.

If I went into that house, there would be no mouth-watering scents coming out of the kitchen, where my mother was constantly cooking and baking. If she wasn't cooking for her family, she would be making something for one town function or another. Or just a little treat for some of the neighbors.

There would be no sounds coming up from the basement, where my father loved to spend many hours tinkering away, carving wood into beautiful furniture that he would sell, or toys that he would then give away to the local children. They loved his wooden toys. And him.

I sank lower into the seat of my car, the feeling of guilt creeping in fast and furious, weighing me down. I wish I had been a better daughter. I wish I would have called them more often, visited them all the time, even without an excuse to do so. I shouldn't have needed an excuse. I wish we had done more things together.

I wish I would have told them that I loved them. I mean, I did tell them, just not as much as I should. And now I deeply regret it. I should have told them every chance I got.

Now it was too late.

The image of their darkened house grew blurry as my eyes filled up with tears. I rested my forehead on my cracked steering wheel and broke down, my body shaking as I sobbed.

When the tears had run dry, I fished out a couple tissues from my purse, dabbing at my eyes and nose as I dialed Dylan's number.

Dylan was my boyfriend. We had been dating off

and on for a few months now. It was nothing serious, but still. I needed him at this moment.

After a few unanswered rings it went to voicemail. Shaking my head in frustration, I sighed and hung up the phone without leaving a message. It would have been pointless, anyway. Dylan never replied when I left any. He rarely answered any texts, either.

Why was I even with him?

Tossing the phone back into my purse, I decided to go visit the only person who always had my back, who always listened and was full of helpful advice. Turning the ignition back on, I backed out of the driveway and headed across town.

"Hey, Gram," I told her, resting my hand on the cold top of her headstone. Vivian Prescott, or Grandma Viv as she was known to me and many others, had died a few years ago from natural causes. I missed her dearly. Not a day went by that I didn't think of or miss her. I think I had always felt closer to her than to anyone else in my family. She had been a huge part of my life. The day she died was the day I truly felt alone. Now, there was a huge hole that had been ripped out of my heart.

Wiping the dead leaves and dried twigs out of the way, I sat down on the ground, resting my back against the stone. "I know it's been a long time, Gram, but I just don't know what to do." I wiped away the fresh tears that had formed. "I don't want to believe this is real. I don't want to be alone," I said, my voice low, barely above a whisper. "How could they be taken away from me? How could all of you be taken from me? It's not fair."

I hugged my knees close to my chest, resting my chin on them while my mind drifted. I wondered if my parents were reunited with Gram up in Heaven, or wherever it was they ended up. I hoped so. I hoped they were all together and happy.

"What do I do, Gram? How can I carry on?" I wish I could hear her answers, feel her warmth as she held me tightly in a hug, doing her best to comfort me. She was the best at that. She was the best at everything. God, I missed her.

The graveyard suddenly filled up with fog. I was so lost in my memories of Gram that by the time I noticed, it was so thick I could barely see two feet in front of me. My heart began racing inside my chest. Scrambling to my feet, I felt my way around the tombstones, looking to find my way out of there.

Soft laughter drifted up out of nowhere, making me feel even more nervous than I already was. I stopped, my heart pounding so hard now that I was sure it was going to fly right out of my chest. Straining my ears, I listened for the sound again, hoping it was as innocent as I first imagined. When it came, I closed my eyes in relief.

It wasn't the sound of any sort of demon or

monster like my mind was telling me it was. Just people laughing, having a good time. Nothing sinister.

Letting out a long breath, I dropped my hand from the musty old tombstone I had been using to prop myself up on and followed the sound. I couldn't explain it, but I felt almost as if I was being pulled towards whatever was making the noise. That, and I was genuinely curious about who would willingly be hanging out in a graveyard, just for the fun of it.

Graveyards aren't fun. They're depressing. And disgusting.

I weaved my way through the fog and around the tombstones until I came upon a faint glowing. Slowly, I crept up near the small crowd that was gathered near a modest bonfire.

Seriously, what was wrong with people? A full-blown party in the middle of one of the most depressing places ever. There were way better places to hold parties. Ones where dead people weren't buried right under your feet.

Crouching behind a large headstone, I watched them, curiosity getting the best of me. I knew I should just turn around and leave, but I couldn't help it. From my hiding spot, they appeared to be rowdy teenagers, getting drunk and having fun out here, away from the prying eyes of adults. I guess I could understand that. But still.

But why the fog? As I pondered this, a crow flew dangerously close to my head. At least I think it was a crow. It had the body and shape of a crow, but it was pure white. I had never seen anything like it before. The feathers, talons, even its beak were bright white. I was so startled by it that I fell backwards against the headstone, a small scream escaping from my throat. I quickly covered my mouth with my hand, hoping the people attending the party hadn't heard me. The last thing I needed was for them to find out I was spying on them. Who knew what would happen to me then? Even though they seemed to be innocently drinking in a graveyard, there was a dark, uneasy sensation in the air. I couldn't shake the feeling that something horrible was going to happen tonight.

"Well, well, well. What do we have here?" A man suddenly materialized out of the fog, standing directly in front of me. He was tall and thin, yet muscular. With the lack of natural light, his eyes looked pure black, with hair to match. I was too afraid to say anything, so I remained silent as he crouched down in front of me to get a better look.

"Come on," he said with a crooked smile. In one swift movement, he had me by the arm and dragged me up and over to his circle of friends.

"What do ya have there, Sergei?" one of the guys asked, prompting hoots and hollers all around. I struggled against my captor, but it only made him hang on tighter. I was sure I was going to have a bruise tomorrow. "Found this lovely little thing hiding behind one of the headstones, spying on us." He flashed that crooked smile again. It made my skin crawl. "So, what do you propose we do with her?"

Fear gripped at me as they shouted out their suggestions.

"Chop her head off!"

"Bury her alive!"

"Rip her heart out!"

Sergei laughed, an evil, gut-twisting sound. "No," he said. "I've got something else in mind. Spying is not okay. Anyone who's caught doing such an act deserves to be punished, don't you think?" he said while staring directly at me. I squirmed under his gaze. My discomfort was amusing for him. This was all just a fun game to him. Sergei cocked his head to the side. "I'm going to have a lot of fun with you. I'm thinking a nice, slow death. Maybe throw in a little torture, for my pleasure, of course," he added, licking his lips slowly.

Fear sent shivers throughout my entire body.

"I wasn't spying," I protested, having finally found my voice again. "I wasn't, I swear," I said to the non-believing crowd. "I didn't ..."

"I don't care," Sergei said, cutting me off. "Whatever it was that you were doing, I don't like it," he growled.

"Sergei! Enough!" A voice bellowed through the air. "Let her go." A figure emerged from the fog, coming straight for him. Sergei let out what sounded like a snarl, yet tightened his grip on my arm even further. The crowd of people scattered as he walked towards Sergei and me, his strides long and purposeful. He had his head held high and shoulders squared. Whoever it was, they meant business.

Stopping inches from Sergei's face, the man repeated himself. "I said—Let. Her. Go." The two men stared each other down for what seemed like an eternity. The air crackled with tension, waves of anger rolling off both of them.

Finally, Sergei backed up a step. "Fine, Nic. Have it your way. As always," he said, throwing me to the ground. "You know, I'm really getting sick and tired of you always ruining our fun," he added before turning around and stalking off into the night. Nic turned to the crowd. "The rest of you had better head home as well. Now." Silently, they obeyed. Most averted their gazes, choosing to keep their eyes on their feet as they made their way out of the graveyard.

Once they were far enough away, Nic waved his hand, and the fog began to disappear.

I shook my head in disbelief. "What—"

"Are you all right?" he asked, his voice now soft and soothing, his body no longer rigid and intimidating. His eyes too were calm, inviting. "He didn't hurt you, did he? Sergei?"

"No, I don't think so. He just held onto my arm a little too tightly, but that was it," I admitted, still trying to process everything that just happened. Nic looked me over carefully, just in case I had missed anything. He knew this Sergei—what would that man have done to me? And those eyes he had … so *black* in that moment. Who—what—was he?

"You're sure you're going to be okay?"

I nodded, touched by this man's concern for me. He had no idea who I was; he didn't have to care about me or what happened to me.

Nic stood almost a foot taller than me. He was thin, but not too thin. You could tell he definitely hit the gym every once in a while. He had unruly brown hair that looked like it had never had a comb run through it. But the thing that really drew me in were his eyes-piercing blue eyes that drew you in. It was unlike any color I had ever seen.

"Good." Nic smiled. He took a step closer to me. Gently, he lifted my chin so I was looking him directly in the eye. "You've had a hard night," he said, his voice low and soothing again. "Why don't you head on home, get cleaned up, and get a good night's rest. Tomorrow's a brand-new day."

I felt a wave of warmth flow through my body. It was gone in a second, so I wasn't sure if I was imagining things or not. Blinking a few times, I studied my surroundings. I was in the graveyard.

How did I get here?

Had I meant to visit the graveyard tonight?

But then I remembered Nic, and what he'd said. "I think I will be heading home," I told him, in a daze. "It really is getting late. So thank you … Nic … for rescuing me and making sure I was all right. Thank you." My voice trailed off.

Nic smiled. "It was my pleasure. Until we meet again," he said mysteriously, taking my right hand and kissing it lightly. I couldn't speak, only stare at him as he made his way out of the graveyard.

Shaking my head to bring myself back to reality, I began to make my way back to my parents' house. Even though it was the last place I wanted to be right now.

CHAPTER TWO

The second Honoria was out of sight, I slipped back into my white crow form. Keeping my distance under the moonlight, I flew from tree to tree, making sure Sergei and his crew kept their word and left her alone.

Once I was certain she was home and safe, I jumped off the branch I was perched on and headed on towards my place.

I had no clue what it was about Honoria, but I felt a strong pull towards her. An attraction like I'd never felt before. I had walked this earth for hundreds of years, yet I never experienced something quite like this before.

I felt a strong need to protect her. Especially after our meeting in the graveyard. The sadness in her eyes floored me, and I found myself wanting to do anything to make her smile.

Why did I feel this way?

Back at the lair where all of us resided, I called everyone to a meeting in the common room.

"Just what the hell went on up there today? What exactly were you thinking?" I asked them, anger rolling off me. Three sets of eyes stared at me, watching as I paced back and forth in front of them. But no one said a single word, just shifted uncomfortably in their seats.

Sergei checked out his hands, inspecting his nails. "Are we just about done here?" he asked in a bored tone.

"No, we are not done," I scoffed. "Why were you hanging out in the graveyard, terrorizing humans?"

He shrugged. "Just having a little fun. Calm down, *Dad*," he said, prompting giggles from the rest.

Rage rose within me, especially when I knew how much Sergei loved all this. He was always picking fights, arguing, complaining about anything and everything. He had a red temper and the world's shortest fuse.

"You know how hard we've worked to keep out of the eyes of humans." I said. "You also know that we have to keep a low profile. You can't be having loud parties out in the open and scaring the humans. Especially the ones who come to pay a visit to their deceased loved ones. Have some respect." I fisted my hands at my sides.

Sergei rolled his eyes, moving to stand up. "Fine," he said, throwing his hands up. "Whatever you say, *Dad*."

I really wished he would stop calling me that. But he knew how much it bugged me and that was why he kept doing it.

The other two had remained quiet throughout the exchange, but I hadn't forgotten about them. I turned to face them both, and they kept their eyes to the floor. "I am extremely disappointed in the two of you. You have never behaved like this before. I know Sergei can be very persuasive, but you can't let him talk you into doing things like this again. It's dangerous. Not only for you, but for all of us. It's important that we stay hidden. Do you understand?"

They both nodded.

"Good, then go on and get some rest," I dismissed them. In a flash, they were both up and out of the room. Both were good people. Sergei just had that way about him. He could basically convince anyone to do anything.

CHAPTER THREE

Honoria

I woke up the next morning in my old room, back at my parents' house. It felt strange. Wrong, even. Especially since the house was cold, dark, lifeless. There would be no home-cooked breakfast and a kiss on the top of my head from my mother. There would be no loving banter with my father as he drank his coffee and read the morning paper.

That thought made it hard to get out of bed. I pulled the blankets closer to my chin and snuggled down into my cocoon. *Do I really have to get up and do anything today?* I couldn't think of a single thing I absolutely needed to do. Meeting with the funeral directors and all that wasn't for another day or two.

After a few more minutes of lounging, I forced myself to get up. The silence was becoming too much to bear. Checking the time on my cell phone, I noticed it was almost noon already. The incident in the graveyard last night must have really drained me, too.

I also noticed there was no missed call—not even a single text message from Dylan. Not that I was surprised. He never cared enough to check in on me.

One of the reasons I had to break up with him.

As I began getting dressed for the day, my mind wandered back to the graveyard. Back to Nic. I didn't know anything about him really, apart from his name. And the fact he had unruly brown hair, and those piercing blue eyes. The kind that felt like they looked directly into your soul. I don't know what it was, or how to explain it. There was just … something about him. Something I wanted to learn more about.

I made my way downstairs and the sight of my father's favorite armchair made me stop in my tracks. He loved that chair. Every morning and every evening after work he'd be there, relaxing in his cozy seat pulled up close to the fireplace. I ran my hands over the worn fabric, memories flooding my mind.

Before bedtime when I was a child, we would sit together here while he read me one of my favorite stories, probably for the thousandth time. Whenever I needed my father, be it for advice, help with something I was having a problem with, or just a comforting hug, I could always find him here.

Now the fabric was cold, unused. Forgotten. Kind of how I felt at the moment.

Wandering into the kitchen wasn't any better. There was no bacon frying in a pan, fresh squeezed orange juice on the counter waiting to be poured into a glass. No pancake batter being stirred or fresh fruit waiting to be cut up. Not even a single piece of silverware lying out on the counter. Everything was cleaned up and put in its place. That's how my parents were. They would make sure everything was spotless before leaving the house, even if it was just to go down the street.

I opened the fridge, but I knew I wouldn't be able to eat anything. I hadn't had much of an appetite since learning of their accident. Instead, I grabbed the bottle of apple juice and poured myself a glass. At least it was something.

Time dragged on. Minutes seemed like hours. The walls began to close in on me, and I was beginning to feel suffocated.

I have to get out of here. Right now.

I got up to retrieve my car keys, leaving my half cup of juice on the table.

I drove around the entire town at least once. Which wasn't hard, considering Glenfall Heights was small. Like, really small. Everyone-up-in-your-business small. I then left the car in the parking lot near the town square, deciding to just take a walk. Nowhere in particular, just to help clear my mind.

As I walked the streets, gazing into the windows of various shops, bakeries, and other businesses, I wondered if I would spot Nic in any of them. I had no idea what I would even say to him if I did run into him. All I knew was that I wanted to see him again. If anything, he was a welcome distraction from thinking about my parents.

And right on cue, as if they could read my mind, I was surrounded by people who wanted to offer their condolences, let me know they were there for me, for whatever it was I might need. A few I didn't even recognize wanted to know exactly what had happened to my parents, and how I was feeling.

I hated it. I knew they meant well, but this was all just too much. Couldn't they see I just wanted to be left alone? I didn't want to stand here and try to answer a million questions I didn't have the answers to. I bit my lip to keep myself from crying.

That suffocating feeling from this morning came flooding back, along with the sudden urge to flee again.

"Excuse me," I said to no one in particular as I began to push my way through the crowd. Once free of their grasp, I picked up my pace. I didn't stop running until I reached the small park at the edge of the woods. This was a place I had spent a lot of time in as a child, visiting with my parents probably at least every other day.

Off to one side of the park, separate from the play area, sat rows of picnic tables, away from all the screams and noises of the children playing on the slides, swings, and various other playground equipment. I slowed down as I got near them, weathering a few odd looks from some of the parents there, and took a seat at a vacant one. My hair was a mess and my face and eyes red and puffy from all the crying I had done. No wonder I was getting so much attention. The kids, all too absorbed in their playing, paid absolutely no attention to me.

I wished the adults in this town would do the same. It was only natural for people to be curious when a tragic accident occurred and want to offer their support, but those who grieve also needed space and time to process everything.

My life had suddenly changed, in a huge way. The last thing I needed right now was to try to answer questions I either didn't know the answers to or didn't even want to think about in the first place. I didn't want to have to play host to a bunch of people who were either genuinely saddened by the death of my parents or who were just nosy and wanted the hot gossip of the day.

I rested my elbows on the worn wooden table, my face hidden in my hands.

I should not have even left the house.

CHAPTER FOUR

Honoria

"We have to stop meeting like this," a voice came from my right side, accompanied by a low laugh, startling me and bringing me out of the depressing spiral I had been sucked into. When I looked to find the owner of the voice to tell them off, to reiterate that I just wanted to be left alone, I couldn't find the words.

A set of piercing blue eyes looked down at me, set in a face framed with unruly brown hair.

Nic.

"I see you're doing better today," he said.

I found myself unable to tear my eyes away. *He's here ... he's really here.*

I took in a steadying breath, trying to get myself together as he took a seat next to me.

"Do you want to talk about it?" he asked, concern and compassion filling his eyes.

I didn't, but something about Nic made me want to open up. I felt safe in his presence, and perhaps not only because of what happened in the graveyard. How could I explain it?

I closed my eyes and sucked in a deep breath before answering him. "It's just... already too much. Everything is. Both of my parents were killed in an accident just recently. I had just spoken with them both. And now, they're gone. I haven't had time to process my feelings about my parents, or even come to terms with their death. I still don't want to believe it happened," I wrapped my arms around myself, staring down at a chipped spot on the surface of the table. "I tried to stay in their house last night but the flood of memories was just too much to bear. Everywhere I looked reminded me of them." I sniffled. "So I thought maybe taking a walk would help clear my mind. But boy, was I wrong." I let out a wry laugh. "All these people trying to show sympathy and I ... I just couldn't handle it. How can I when I can't even make sense of this myself?"

Nic moved to put his arms around me as fresh tears fell in streaks down my face. I had thought I was all cried out by now. I accepted his touch and leaned into him, resting my head on his shoulder as the tears flowed freely. He had been so kind to me, sitting there patiently as I rambled on about my problems, never interrupting me or making me feel like I was overreacting. Maybe I was, maybe I wasn't. I have no clue how one was supposed to act when a loved one died. I'd never experienced this before. I was just trying to take it one day at a time.

"I am so sorry to hear of the passing of your parents," Nic said, rubbing his hand up and down my arm. He smelled like cedar and Asian sandalwood. The combination was comforting, and oddly sexy. "I know you're tired of everyone offering," he continued, "but if there's anything you need, I'm here for you."

"Why?" I asked, sniffling again. "I mean, you barely know me." The second the words left my mouth, I instantly regretted them. Here he was, being super nice to me, and I was questioning him. I had thought about him all day, he finally showed up to comfort me, and I went and said something like this. I shook my head, messy hair bouncing around my shoulders. "I'm sorry, I didn't mean that. I ..."

"It's okay." Nic waved his hand in the air, cutting me off. "I get what you mean." He pulled his arm from around me and straightened up in his seat, turning to face me. With one gentle finger, he lifted up my chin so I was looking him in his eyes. Up close I could see they were more of an icy blue. I could get lost in them forever. "Listen to me," he began. "You are going through something major in your life right now. It's okay to be scared, or maybe a little lost. And it's also okay to want to pull back and be alone sometimes. It's a lot to process and deal with. But please, try to remember not to push everyone away. So you'll have someone there for you when you're ready. And if you want, I will be here whenever you need."

That last comment almost sent me crying again. How was it that this beautiful man I had just briefly met yesterday could come to care about me so much? Why was it him, above anyone else, that I wanted to talk to? Nic had already gotten me to open up to him, when everyone else in the town, the people I'd grown up with and had practically known all my life, made me want to run and hide.

"Thank you," I whispered. I couldn't bring myself to speak louder than a whisper for fear of breaking down again. I really appreciated Nic and everything he was trying to do for me. Part of me knew he was right—I would need someone eventually, when I was ready. It was just hard for me not to push everyone away at this time.

Hurt them before they could hurt me.

I wiped the tears from my face, then tried to smooth my hair down the best I could. Hopefully Nic didn't mind that I looked like a puffy mess that just rolled out of bed, but I couldn't help feeling a little self-conscious.

"You look fine," he said, as if reading my thoughts. I laughed, for the first time in a while, and it felt good.

"Thanks," I said. "I don't usually look like this though." I wasn't one to always throw on a ton of makeup and do my hair, or wear trendy clothes. But at least I would look presentable.

"Are you sure you're going to be okay?" Nic asked me again. I nodded.

"I just need some time to pull myself together," I admitted. It sounded a lot easier than it really was. I looked like a mess on the outside, but inside was a completely different story. A huge storm of emotions whirled around in there, with no end in sight.

"Well, if you ever need me, I'll be around." He pushed himself up from the table. Before I could ask him what that meant, he vanished.

He simply disappeared into thin air.

The next few days flew by in a blur. I had to meet with attorneys and funeral directors and everyone else to discuss the plans for their burial, inheritance matters, financial matters, and other things, none of which I could remember. Thankfully, everything was written down for me in the thick manila folder that lay untouched on the dining room table.

The neighbors began stopping by one by one. It was almost worse than when I was ambushed out on the streets. At least there I could—and did—run away. This time, I was trapped in my own home. My parents' home. And I couldn't even leave if I wanted to. Everyone brought over food that was either cooked or ready to be baked or otherwise heated. Most left instructions taped to the top of the dish. Others rattled them off, expecting me to remember them.

The majority of the food would sit uneaten in the fridge or cupboard. I wasn't sure how long I would be staying in Glenfall Heights. I needed a solid plan I didn't have yet.

After the last guest left for the night, I breathed a sigh of relief. Stepping onto the back porch, I dug my cell phone out of my pocket and dialed Dylan's number. As usual, it went straight to voicemail. I had no idea why I thought he'd answer, or why it would be different this time.

Tears slid down my face. A death in the family and he still couldn't act like a loving boyfriend. Not that he really ever acted that way. Still, one would think he would at least pretend to care right now.

I wiped the tears from my face, and turned to head inside.

Tomorrow, I would say my final goodbyes to my parents.

CHAPTER FIVE

Nic

I volunteered to come with Honoria as she met with all the lawyers, funeral directors, and everyone else she needed to connect with that week. No one should have to be alone for something like that.

Throughout every meeting, she would just sit there staring at whoever was talking, her eyes vacant. She would nod along but I doubt she actually ever heard a word they were saying. I made sure to ask questions and write everything down for her to address later. I made sure she wouldn't miss a thing.

It hurt me to see her like this. So sad and broken, not knowing what to do. I didn't even know how to comfort her. All I knew was that she needed someone there by her side, and I had no intention of leaving.

"I'm sorry I made you do all the work," Honoria said, dropping down on the couch with a loud sigh. "I should have been paying attention. I'm sorry," she said sadly.

I set down the cup of tea I'd made for her on the coffee table and sat down beside her. "I don't mind," I told her sincerely. "I wanted to be there for you."

Without a word, she closed her eyes and leaned against my chest. I could feel her body move with her soft sobs.

I held her until her tears dried up and she announced she was ready for bed. Once she was settled, I quietly did the dishes for her and straightened up the downstairs.

I stretched my arms over my head, feeling the exhaustion of the week. I forgot how tiring it was to care all the time. How did humans do it?

Honoria was stronger than she gave herself credit for.

Turning off the lights, I got comfortable on the couch, falling asleep almost instantly.

CHAPTER SIX

Honoria

The entire town turned up for the funeral. Looking around at all their faces, I could see just how much my parents had meant to this small town. Almost everyone stepped forward to tell a short story of how they had impacted their lives. A lot of them mentioned the wooden toys my father made for their children, and how they treasured them.

Ladies would talk about the book clubs or the knitting evenings they shared with my mother. It seemed like every night she had something different going on.

Though the tears never stopped flowing, their stories touched me, making me feel a little lighter.

"Are you just about done here?" Dylan asked

impatiently from beside me. He had surprised me by coming out here just in time for the funeral.

Everyone had gone back to the comfort of their homes, the service having finished and the rain now beginning to fall. Dylan and I were the last two remaining. I just couldn't bring myself to leave yet. I wasn't ready.

"I'm not ready," I told him, my voice barely above a whisper. My throat felt raw from all the crying I had been doing.

Dylan scoffed, kicking rocks around with his feet. "Well, how much more time do you need? It's raining, and freezing. You've already said goodbye and they're in the ground."

I turned to face him, mouth hanging wide open. I could not believe the words that had just come out of his mouth. Dylan had always been fairly insensitive, but this was crossing a line. "I'm sorry that I am inconveniencing you. I'm sorry that the death of my parents is inconveniencing you," I said as I took a step towards him. I fisted my hands at my side, as I'd never been so angry with him. "Our entire relationship you've never shown an ounce of emotion, never once even pretended to care about me or anything concerning my life. At first, I thought I needed to give you more time … to give *us* more time. Now though, I don't know why I even put up with you anymore. Out of habit, maybe."

Dylan just stood there, no emotion whatsoever

showing on his stupid face. He never said a word to defend himself or try to explain anything, make things right. He never did anything.

No surprise there.

Raising my hands in the air in both frustration and defeat, I huffed out a huge breath. "You know what?" I shook my head. "I'm done, like I should have been ages ago. Done with you and this sham of a relationship. I want you to leave."

"Whatever," he scoffed. "You don't mean it. You and I both know it. How many times have we had this fight?"

Too many. Way too many. "I don't deserve this. I really don't. I deserve better. You and I both know it," I said, mocking his earlier tone. I was being a little childish but right now I really didn't care. I'd had enough of him and his lack of caring.

"I stood by your side no matter how crappy your treatment of me. Stayed with you when you did nothing but ignore me, even pretending I didn't exist at times, if you were with the wrong crowd. I supported you when you wanted to quit or change careers every few months. I have loved you, cared for you, supported you, both emotionally and financially. And what have you given me in return? Nothing!" I practically screamed.

My chest heaved as my body filled with rage. Rage at him and at me, for having put up with this emotional abuse for so long. I felt stupid. Numb. But mostly, I wanted to scream. My blood boiled, keeping me warm even though I was being pelted with freezing drops of rain.

"If there was any day that I could have used your love and support, it was today. And you ruined it. You ruined us! I want you gone. Out of my parents' house, out of my town, and out of my life!"

"You don't mean that," he said again, a little less sure this time.

"Oh, I really do," I said through gritted teeth. "I want you long gone by the time I get home tonight. And I never want to see you again." Before he could choke out a reply, I turned away from him and walked up beside my parents' gravesites. I didn't watch to see if he'd left. I meant the part about never seeing him again.

After a few seconds of silence, I heard the sound of shoes squelching in the puddles in the grass and someone made their way over to me. "I said leave me alone, Dylan." I swiped at my face, the anger now gone, leaving me feeling cold and drained of all energy. I had no fight left in me.

He didn't answer, but the footsteps got closer. I opened my mouth to say something else, but stopped when I was suddenly under the shelter of an umbrella. I hadn't realized just how chilly the air had gotten until I was no longer being pelted with raindrops.

The scent of cedar and Asian sandalwood filled the air and my heart stopped. "I thought you could use this," Nic said softly. He shifted beside me as he took off his jacket and slid it around my shoulders. I hugged it tightly, relishing the warmth.

Nic, my ever-present knight in shining black armor, always coming to my rescue. That's how I like to think about him, because every time I'd seen him he was wearing all-black clothing. It seemed that no matter where I was or what was happening, he knew I needed him and he was there.

"Thank you," I replied, grateful for not only the warmth of his jacket but just for him being here. His was a calming presence after my blow out with Dylan. "Have you been here long?" I ask slowly, wondering if he'd caught me yelling and making a fool out of myself.

Nic cleared his throat, shifting from one foot to the other. "I've actually been here the whole time. I wasn't sure if you wanted me here. And then I saw your … boyfriend," he said the word like it was poison, "so I stayed hidden behind the large oak tree behind us. But I wanted to be here for you."

My heart warmed at his words. I had almost forgotten what it was like to have someone care for you. "Dylan is not my boyfriend," I said, trying to hide my anger. "I ended things."

"I heard. I am so sorry. I wasn't trying to eavesdrop," he added quickly when I gave him a face, "But your voice was raised and carried on the wind. And I didn't want to leave until I knew you were safe.

There was that warm feeling once more. "Thank you," I said again. Not knowing what else to say, I leaned into him, laying my head on his shoulder. I breathed in the scent of Nic as he shifted the umbrella to his right hand so he could put his left arm around me. Just being around him made me feel both safe and comfortable.

For as long as I needed, he just held me, letting me silently say goodbye to my mother and father.

CHAPTER SEVEN

Honoria

Dylan had taken my car. I'd been stupid enough to let him hang onto the keys, because the dress I wore had no pockets and I didn't bring a purse. Good thing Glenfall Heights was a small town, because I had no other choice but to walk back home. Nic kept me company the entire way, holding the umbrella steadily over the two of us. We walked in silence down the vacant sidewalks, our feet splashing in the many unavoidable puddles. I was already soaked through to the bone though, so it didn't really bother me. This was typical weather in this town, anyway. You got used to the doom and gloom feel. After a while, it didn't even seem that bad.

The closer we got to my house, the more I dreaded it. Dylan, not wanting to pay for a hotel room, stayed with me. I mean, it did make sense. He took over one of the guest rooms—staying the night in the same room as me was never an option to him.

Which was fine with me. Now I just hoped he would respect my wishes and be gone by the time I got there.

"Do you want me to go ahead and make sure he's gone?" Nic asked me, as if reading my mind. He did that a lot.

"Yes, please," I answered. I didn't care if I sounded weak. I just didn't want to face Dylan. Honestly, I had no idea what I would have done without Nic the past few days.

All the lights seemed to be on in the house. Nic motioned for me to wait on the porch while he went in and dealt with Dylan. I stood next to the front door, but far enough away that if it swung open, it wouldn't hit me. Hearing voices, I strained my ears, but they were muffled and I couldn't pick up a single word that was spoken.

Heavy footsteps indicated that they were heading toward the door. I backed up a few steps, even though I knew I would be safe. Sure enough, it was swung open with so much force, it bounced off the side of the house. Luckily, it didn't seem to leave a mark.

My heart pounded as Dylan turned to face me. "I hope you know what you're doing," he growled, venom dripping from his voice. "Once I leave here, I am never coming back. You will never see my face again," he said. He stared at me as if expecting me to say something.

But I'd said all I needed to back at the funeral.

"You're gonna regret this," he spat as he walked to the end of the driveway. He looked both right and then left before lobbing his gaze between my car and me.

"Bus station is a few miles down that way," Nic told him, pointing down the street before he could ask me for a ride.

Hitching up his bag, Dylan muttered something under his breath and took off, walking out of my life, hopefully for good.

I breathed a sigh of relief once he was out of sight. "Come on," Nic said, putting his arm around my shoulder and guiding me into the house. "Let's get you inside. You really should dry off and get warm."

I had completely forgotten about the weather and the soaking wet clothes clinging to my body.

While I showered and put on clean, dry clothes, Nic found his way around the kitchen. I could hear dishes clattering as I walked down the stairs to the first floor.

"I hope this is okay," he said when he spotted me in the doorway. He pulled out a chair for me and I took a seat. Nic quickly grabbed and placed in front of me a bowl of vegetable soup that he had heated up, along with a cup of tea. "I thought these would help warm you up."

"Thank you. I haven't had a single bite to eat all day," I admitted. I had been too busy with the funeral and Dylan and having the entire town trying to comfort me. More often than not, I had to be the one to comfort them.

Nic flashed me a look of worry, telling me to eat at least a little bit. I obeyed, as my stomach growled loudly. After making sure I was in fact eating, he turned to finish cleaning the dishes he had used to make the soup and tea.

"You don't have to do that," I said around a mouthful. "I can do those later."

"I don't mind," he replied with a wave of his hand. "You've had a long, trying day. You eat and take it easy. I got this."

I wasn't used to being taken care of like this. It was nice. Really nice. I watched as Nic cleaned the dishes and wiped the counters. His black button-up shirt fit him just right, and he had the sleeves rolled up to avoid getting them wet with dishwater. His hair had that fresh out of the shower look to it. Heat crept up my neck and face, and I quickly lowered my eyes to my bowl before he caught me staring.

After I finished eating, I brought my dishes over to the sink. Our fingers brushed up against each other's and his felt cold, I assumed from the dishwater. Turning my head quickly so he couldn't see the how the touch affected me, I made my way back to the table and sat down. I was more exhausted than I thought, but I wasn't quite ready to go to sleep yet. I wanted to spend as much time with Nic as I could.

"So," I said, not really sure what to say next, "tell me about yourself."

Nic stopped doing the dishes and turned to look at me. "All right. What would you like to know?" He laughed.

"I don't know," I admitted. "Tell me anything, everything. Who is Nic, … um, I'm sorry, I don't even know your last name?" I felt awful about that. Nic had saved me countless times already, and I hadn't even thought to ask him what his last name was.

"It's Blackwood," he answered, wiping the soapy water off his hands on a towel.

"Nicolas Blackwood," I sounded it out.

Nic laughed again as he joined me at the table.

"Any brothers or sisters?" I asked, trying to keep the conversation going.

"Nope. I'm an only child, like you." He smiled. The smile quickly faded away and his expression grew serious. It made me nervous somehow. "Before we get too much into the questions, I have something to confess about myself. Something important," he began. He shifted uncomfortably in his seat. "I've never really told anyone about this before. Not anyone … human before anyway."

Anyone human? What the hell did that mean? My heart began pounding wildly in my chest as my mind raced with the possibilities of what Nic had meant by that.

Nic stood and began pacing the kitchen. "I've never

told anyone this, but I like you. I've felt drawn to you since the day we met," he admitted.

I let out an uneasy laugh. "Even though every time we've been together, it's been so you could save me?" I teased. Maybe he was just into the whole damsel-in-distress thing.

"Even then," he answered. All traces of humor had vanished from his face. "You're going through a hard time, and I get that. But I like *you*, the woman behind all that pain and sadness. And I would like to get to know you more.

"I feel I can't do that if there's this huge secret hanging between us" He let out a long breath and sat back down near me. "This is hard for me," he apologized, "but I can't have you finding out any other way. I want there to be trust between us. So here goes … Honoria, I'm a vamp …"

Before he could finish what he was saying, he was interrupted by the sound of glass breaking. Nic was up out of his seat and into the living room before I could register the fact that he had even moved. "Stay back!" he yelled as I stepped into the doorway to the living room. One of the large windows facing the street was shattered, glass shards covered the floor, and the small end table where my father's reading glasses and a stack of books still lay was now shattered. Outside, I could hear shouting.

"What is it?" I whispered, panic filling me.

He carefully walked over the bits of glass to the

window. "Your ex is back," he answered, peering out into the night. "Don't," he held up a hand as I took a step towards him. "It's not safe. He has another brick in his hands."

I shook my head in anger. I couldn't believe this was happening. Throughout our relationship, he'd given me all the space I wanted, even if I didn't want it. I hardly ever saw him. We never went out together in public. I mean, the guy wouldn't even answer my calls and left my texts 'unread.' Yet here he was, throwing bricks though my living room window, trying to get my attention.

What the hell?

"Do you think I should go talk to him? See what he wants?" I knew it was a stupid question the second the words flew out of my mouth.

"I don't think that's a good idea," Nic said. He walked over and put his hands on my arms. "Why don't I take care of it for you?" His voice became low and soothing, and that warm feeling flooded through my body again. I simply nodded, having lost the ability to speak. Being so close to Nic had that effect on me.

After he went outside to confront Dylan, I snuck closer to the window, hoping to hear what was going on.

"What the hell are you doing here?" Nic asked him.

"I could ask you the same question," Dylan spat back. "I want to see my girlfriend."

"You don't have a girlfriend anymore, man. And she

doesn't want to see you." Nic stood tall, crossing his arms and squaring his shoulders. "I think you should leave."

Dylan marched right up to him, getting in his face. "I don't think I should." He cocked his head to the side as an attempt to look intimidating. There was nothing intimidating about that man, especially when he was standing next to Nic. Dylan looked small, almost childlike. "And you certainly don't get to tell me what to do. Now, I want to see Honoria. And you are not going to stop me," he said, poking Nic in the chest with each word.

"Again, she doesn't want to see you," he said, swatting Dylan's hand away. "And don't ever touch me again." Nic balled up his fists, but kept them by his sides. He stood over Dylan, staring him down, as if challenging him.

"There you go again, trying to tell me what to do." Dylan threw his hands up in the air. Nic just stood there, his face scrunched up in anger. When he didn't get a response, Dylan tried again. "What do you care anyway, huh? It's not like you mean anything to her." He turned to look towards the window. I quickly ducked out of the way, praying he hadn't noticed me.

"Honoria only cares about one thing, and that's herself. She could never care for you. She's selfish and heartless. Useless."

Tears slid down my face, hot and fast. I swiped at them, angry at myself for letting him make me feel this way. Not wanting to hear any more, I silently moved away from the window, careful not to step on any glass, and slumped down on the couch. I trusted that Nic would take care of him for me.

I jumped when the door opened a few minutes later. It was only Nic though, and my heart began to calm down. "Is he …"

"He's gone, don't worry," Nic assured me in his soothing voice. "I doubt he'll be coming back here. You'll be safe."

"I don't feel safe," I admitted, hugging my knees to my chest. I hated feeling this way. Why couldn't I stand up for myself? My sadness was quickly turning to anger. At Dylan. At myself. I was more than capable of putting Dylan in his place when needed. Or anyone else who needed it, for that matter. Why my confidence seemed shattered and I felt weak was beyond me.

Nic took a seat next to me, the cushion sagging under his weight. "Well, I'm here. For as long as you need me."

I leaned over and rested my head on his shoulder, his comforting scent filling the air. It didn't take long for the weight of the day to overcome me. As much as I tried, I couldn't fight the tiredness washing over me. I closed my eyes, falling into a deep sleep.

CHAPTER EIGHT

Honoria

I woke up with an anxious feeling in the pit of my stomach. Last night I dreamt of fog and fangs, blood and white crows. My head was pounding to match my drumming heart. Then it all came back to me—Nic trying to tell me something, Dylan breaking my window, saying goodbye to my parents one last time. I pulled the covers tighter to my chest. I had no desire to get out of bed today.

Speaking of which, how did I get here? I didn't remember walking up the stairs last night, let alone changing and crawling into bed. Last thing I remembered was falling asleep on Nic's shoulder.

Movement in the corner of my room startled me. Slowly, my eyes traveled to the corner, where a dark figure lay. As my eyes focused, I breathed a sigh of relief. It was only Nic. He must have fallen asleep in my chair last night.

"You sleep well?" he asked through a yawn.

I nodded, rubbing the sleep out of my eyes. "I did. I had a really weird dream though. Did I wake you?"

"No, no. I've kind of been awake for a few minutes," he said, rubbing the sleep out of his eyes. Sounded like a lie to me. "Tell me about the dream you had."

"It was nothing, really," I waved my hand dismissively. "It was mostly about, uh, vampires, I think." I laughed awkwardly, feeling stupid mentioning it.

Nic straightened up in the armchair. "That's probably my fault."

"Why?" I was thoroughly confused.

"Because of what I started to tell you yesterday." Nic sat on the edge of the chair, looking me directly in the eyes.

The expression on his face was so serious, it made my heart beat faster. I stared at him in silence, waiting for him to continue.

"Last night," he cleared his throat, "you were asking about me, wanting to know more about who I am."

"Yes."

"Well, I'm a vampire."

"You're a what?"

"A..." He hesitated. "A vampire."

My heart stopped. I looked him in the eyes again,

searching for any sign that he was joking, but his face remained serious.

I took in a slow, deep breath to process this new information. "Okay," I said slowly, not really knowing what else to say. "A vampire. Really?"

"Yes." Nic stood up straighter, bracing himself for the fear and loathing that he was sure was headed his way. He hadn't told many humans that he was a vampire, but those he did quickly turned on him, fearing who he was. What he was. And that fear would turn to hate. Hating him because he hid the truth, hating him simply for the fact that he wasn't human. But he was ready this time. As much as he didn't want Honoria to hate him, she needed to know the truth about him. Hiding it would only make things worse.

Nic went on, talking about his family history and how he became a vampire. What his life has been like since then. But I barely heard a word that he said. My mind was racing all over the place, not sure what to think. What to believe.

"So what do you think?" He asked.

"Honestly, I'm not too sure," I admitted. "It's a lot to take in." Nic nodded. My heart was beating so hard it almost hurt, and my hands began to shake. I slowly moved to hide them under my blanket before he could see.

"If this is too much for you, I can leave. At least until you're ready to see me again," he offered.

"No," I lied. "It's ok."

Was it okay though? Was I crazy to stay here, with a vampire sitting in my room? I didn't know if I should be running and screaming, fearing for my life, or if everything was going to be okay.

But then again, this was Nic we were talking about.

Nic moved from the chair to sit on the edge of my bed. "And you're not frightened of me?" he asked softly.

I shook my head. "No. Should I be?"

"You have no reason to fear me," he assured me, his eyes never leaving mine. "I promise, I will never hurt you. I care about you too much."

I knew in my heart that he was telling the truth. I have been an absolute mess ever since I arrived back in Glenfall Heights. It's just been one thing after another and each time, Nic stuck by my side, comforted me and dried my tears. He saved me from Dylan's attacks and even stayed with me to make sure I was okay. I already owed him so much.

"And about your questions, I will tell you anything you want to know. I have nothing to hide."

"Thank you. I just … I don't know." I shifted on my bed. "It's kind of exciting, I guess." I laughed awkwardly. "I have always believed in vampires, ever since I was a little girl. Always wanted to see one in real life. And now, you're telling me that not only are they real but there's one sitting in my room. On my bed. It doesn't seem real."

"It's real, I promise you. I'm real," Nic said, his voice low. The way he looked at me right now made my cheeks burn. It took everything I had not to jump over the bed and kiss him. He smiled briefly and turned away, as if hearing my mind.

I decided to just come right out and ask. "Hey, can vampires read minds?"

"Some can. It depends on how old they are, how well fed they are, and what type of blood they've fed on."

"Type?' Do blood types make a difference?

"Yeah, human or animal," he replied. "We can survive on animal blood, but it's the blood of humans that gives us energy, enhances our senses and abilities. Not everyone has the same abilities, either."

Speaking of blood … "Aren't you supposed to be all cold and stuff? Your skin, I mean."

Nic laughed at my question. "Not really, no. Drinking human blood, or even just eating warm food gives us the illusion of having a warm, normal body," he explained.

Makes sense, I suppose. Although, there was nothing abnormal about Nic's body. Like the rest of him, it was perfect.

"Can you read minds?" More specifically, my mind.

"I can." He smirked. I looked down at bed, too embarrassed by some of the thoughts I'd had about Nic. "Don't worry." He lifted my chin up to look at him. "Your secrets are safe with me. Promise."

"Thanks," I mumbled. "So, are there a lot more of you here? Vampires, I mean."

Nic nodded, staring out the window as he answered. "There are a few of us here. We all live together, and pretty much keep to ourselves. Not a lot of humans know of our existence, and we like to keep it that way. For our safety."

"So why did you tell me?"

"I trust you." He turned his attention back to me. "I have no reason not to."

"Because you've read my mind?" I teased.

"Partly," he admitted. He looked mortified.

I moved closer to him. "Hey, it's okay. Yes, you listened to my private thoughts, which wasn't the best thing to do, but I understand. It's okay." I mean, I sort of understood. I didn't know if vampires could just tune out or not listen to someone's thoughts. For all I knew, they just heard voices or whispers or whatever all day long. That would drive me crazy. "So, is it safe for you to be around humans for an extended period of time?" I asked.

"It is," he answered quickly. "Over the years, we've learned to control our cravings. Bourbon helps tremendously with that." He smiled. "Vampires can't get drunk. But the alcohol helps keep the blood cravings at bay."

"And what about the sun? You walk around in it just like any other normal person."

"We have these." He held up his hand. On his finger was a thin, silver band, almost like a wedding ring. "Black onyx. It has protection and grounding properties and protects the vampires wearing it from the sun's harmful rays. Not everyone has a ring. Some chose a necklace, bracelet, even earrings."

"Why'd you choose a ring?" I was curious.

Nic shrugged. "Seemed less likely for me to lose it, I guess."

I nodded. Just then my stomach growled, loudly, ruining the moment. "Let's go downstairs," he said with a grin. "I can cook you something to eat real quick."

He headed to the kitchen so I could change out of my pajamas. Not caring too much what I looked like at the moment, I threw on the first clean pair of jeans and t-shirt I could find. It had already started raining so I also grabbed a sweater to throw on top.

I was quickly reminded of the events of last night as I stepped into the living room. A few bits of glass covered various surfaces and the wind was blowing through the parts of the window Dylan had smashed.

"I should have taken care of that last night." Nic came up behind me. "I'm sorry I didn't. I was worried about you, and then you fell asleep and ..."

I waved my hand in the air. "It's fine. It's my responsibility anyways," I said. "My house, my ex. Therefore, my mess."

"You don't have to do this alone." He put his hand on my shoulder. "Any of this. You know I'm here for you. I'm not going anywhere, not until you kick me out." I will admit it was nice to have someone who cared about me so much. It wasn't something I was used to, though. People had a tendency to push me away or ignore me. Not that I didn't do my fair share of the same. Hurt them before they have a chance to hurt you, right?

"I can't stay here," I suddenly admitted. "There's too much—the memories, Dylan, the destruction and hurt he caused." Tears began to fall down my face and I shook my head. "At least not for a while."

Nic took me in his arms, and I didn't hold back. I cried for all the losses I'd felt over the past few days. Weeks? Years? I didn't know anymore, for time didn't make sense to me right then. All the pain, heartache, frustration, anger. I just let it all out.

"How about you come stay with me for a while?" Nic offered once the flood of tears seemed to dry up. "At least until you feel safe enough to come back here."

"Will the others be okay with me staying there?" I sniffled. He did mention that all the vampires of Glenfall Heights lived together.

"They should be. For the most part." That didn't sound very reassuring.

"Should I be worried?"

Nic shook his head. "I don't think you have anything to worry about. It's just … you've actually met some of the vampires I live with. At the graveyard."

My mind flashed back to the group that had terrorized me the night I tried to visit my grandmother. "That was not the best night." I gave a large exhale.

"No," he agreed. "Sergei would be the one to look out for. Not that he's dangerous or anything," he added quickly. "He just has a temper and doesn't think too fondly of humans. But I will explain to him how important you are to me and that you are off limits. You'll be completely safe."

So, after a few minutes of thinking it over, I agreed to go stay with Nic for a while. Living with a bunch of vampires was the last thing I expected to ever do, but there I was. It did seem safer than staying at the house, where Dylan knew I would be. I wasn't sure if he was still in town or if he would try anything else, but I didn't really want to stick around to find out. Nic assured me that he would never find me at his place, and that he would also keep an eye on my parents' home for me, until it was time for me to go back.

CHAPTER NINE

Nic

I really hoped I was doing the right thing by inviting Honoria to stay with us. I still felt the overwhelming need to comfort and protect her. And this would be a whole lot easier to do with her so close.

I had to admit, I was somewhat doing this for selfish reasons. I wanted nothing more than to be able to spend as much time as possible with her. She also shouldn't be staying in that house alone, not with her crazy ex running around.

My blood boiled at the thought of Dylan. I wish I hadn't been so easy on him. If Honoria hadn't been there, I sure as hell would have ripped him a new one.

Literally. Men like him didn't deserve to live. I could have killed him right then and there, saving a lot of women a lot of trouble. But then what would Honoria have thought of me? I didn't want her to think of me as some sort of monster.

No one should treat a woman, or anyone for that matter, the way that monster did. It made me wonder, if that was how he treated her in public, what went on when no one was looking?

I looked over at her as we walked through the town. The day was grey and downcast, matching her mood. She watched the ground sadly, her entire world continuously changing in front of her. I wanted to take her in my arms, comfort her, make her feel like everything was all right, even for a few minutes. I wanted to take away her pain, make her forget all about it.

I honestly could do that—make her forget all the pain. Vampires had that power. The last thing I wanted to do was add to her woes.

I just hoped the others would feel the same way.

CHAPTER TEN

Honoria

After grabbing a quick sandwich at a deli, Nic led me back to the graveyard, arms loaded with a few bags of my clothing and various other belongings I didn't want to leave behind. "Uh, why are we back here?" I asked, scanning the area for any hidden attackers.

Nic looked around, making sure no one could hear him. "We uh … we live here."

"In the cemetery?" I asked, a little too loudly.

"Yes, now please keep your voice down." He scanned the area again.

My hand flew to my mouth. "I am so sorry. I wasn't thinking."

He shrugged me off. "It's okay. Just please be a little more careful. We don't want to be … found out."

"Got it."

We headed down to the back of the graveyard—a part I had never been to before. Not that I spent much time hanging out in graveyards. He led me to a row of vestibule mausoleums. Three of them, side by side, like miniature morbid houses. All these years, I had no idea these existed here.

"Come on," he motioned, walking to the structure in the center. He held open the heavy stone door, and I hesitantly walked inside. Candles illuminated the small space, which had three coffins on each side, carefully sitting in the shelves carved out of the stone walls. The whole place felt cold and depressing, and it gave me the chills.

Walking over to one of the coffins, Nic reaching behind it and pushed a hidden button. I heard something click, and then part of the stone floor began to shift, giving way to steps leading down into darkness.

"After you," Nic gestured.

"You really do live underground, huh?" I tried to laugh but it got caught in my throat. Taking a deep breath, I headed down the stairs, hoping Nic hadn't caught on to just how nervous I was.

As soon as he joined me, the stone floor above us shifted back into place. "Here it is," he announced proudly. "Home sweet home."

Once my eyes adjusted to the darker atmosphere, I took it all in. Candles were lit all around, seemingly the only source of light. Some looked to be flameless candles, mixed in with real ones.

"They're to help with our eyesight," he whispered, leaning in. "Vampires have sensitive eyes and the gentle glow of a flame is better for us."

I didn't think I'd ever get used to the whole mind reading thing.

From our spot by the stairs, I could see what looked like tunnels running in every direction, with doors every so often. It reminded me of an apartment building, or a hotel.

"Okay, so here are the basics," Nic said, setting my belongings down on the floor. "As you can see, there are hallways leading every which way. Each vampire has their own room, sort of like their own little apartment. Only six of us live here permanently right now. You'll meet them all very soon," he assured me. "There's me, you've met Sergei, and keep an eye on the shadows—Shade often sticks to them, literally. That's how he earned that nickname, actually." He laughed.

"What's his real name?'

He stopped and thought for a moment. "You know, we've called him Shade for so long that I actually can't remember. He has his own onyx ring, so he can walk in the sun—he just chooses not to. We have two Bloodlings, Cody and Selene, and—"

"Bloodlings?" I interrupted him.

"That's what we call new vampires."

"Interesting."

That made Nic smile. "I think you'll really like them. Selene is a little older than Cody. Only about a year or so in vampire terms of aging, that is. She never lets him forget it, either. And this," he turned and led me to a cot that was hidden from my view, "is Henrick Fontana."

"You can call me Henri," the older gentleman sitting on the cot told me. "Everyone does. I think it makes me sound less old." He winked.

"I saved the best for the last," Nic said. "You're going to love Henri. He's always full of stories, aren't you?"

"Boy, am I ever!" Henri perked up. "I've been around a lot longer than most everyone here. I certainly was human a lot longer than you young folk." He chuckled.

"I bet there's a story in that." I took a seat next to Henri on his cot. It creaked a little as it accepted my weight.

Henri reminded me of my grandpa, the one that was buried right next to Gram up in the cemetery. He had the kindest, softest blue eyes I had ever seen and thinning grey hair, yet none of the wrinkles you'd expect to see on someone his age.

Henri smiled, but it didn't quite reach his eyes. "There is a story, all right, but it doesn't have the happiest of endings, I'm afraid."

"You don't have to tell me if you don't want to," I told him, despite being curious.

Henri sat back, making himself comfortable. "No

dear, it's all right." He shook his head. "Sad as it may be, I love to tell my stories. Especially when they are about my Mae. Mae was the love of my life," he said, a far off look in his eyes. "We met when we were young, and it was pure love at first sight. At least for me." His eyes glistened over. "May gave me a hard time in the beginning. I think she liked the chase. I wore her down though, all right. We had an amazing life together, filled with love. We didn't have much. But as long as we had each other," he shook his head, "that was all we needed."

"We were quite old when we first learned about the vampires. You heard all kinds of stories but you believed they never had any truth to them. Once the rumors began that we had a couple in our very own town, May and I got quite curious. It seemed romantic, back then. The thought of being a vampire together, getting to be with each other literally forever. Never having to worry about getting old and dying, or catching some disease or other sickness. We would never have to lose each other. What's not to love?" Henri shrugged.

"So, Mae and I made plans to track down the vampires and have them turn us as soon as possible, so we could begin our new lives together. Our new forever."

Henri let out a long sigh before continuing, and I could feel my chest begin to tighten. "Mae left to say her goodbyes to her friends and family, because once you're a vampire you can't really live with or be around your human family anymore, and we were to meet up at a certain time with the vampires." His voice was sounding low now. "So she stayed with her siblings, one last time, and wouldn't you know it—the war started." He paused then, his face taking on a sad mien. "I couldn't get a hold of her to make sure she was safe and alive, so I figured my best option would be to stick to our plan, meet up at our spot, and hope I would see my Mae waiting there for me.

"But she wasn't there. I held off for as long as I could but those vampires were not very patient. I didn't blame them, so without my Mae, I was turned, in hopes that I would still be able to find her and we could get her transition started soon after. But she never made it. None of her family did."

My heart broke for Henri. I scooted closer and put my arms around him. He didn't shed a tear, but held on tightly for a few moments.

"I'm so sorry." I wiped the tears from my eyes. "I can't imagine what you must have felt." I mean, I kind of did, having just lost both my parents. But losing the love of your life was entirely different.

"The worst pain I have ever experienced," he admitted. "I miss her terribly, each and every day. But if I hadn't gone through with it, I wouldn't have met Nic and everyone else. They have been with me through it all. They're my family."

I looked over at Nic, who beamed proudly at the old

man. "Life around here wouldn't be the same without you, Henri. We all love you."

"Hey! What the hell do you think you're doing here?" a voice growled from the shadows. Sergei charged at me, and I jumped back on the cot until my back hit the wall. I was trapped.

Nic quickly stood up and got in his way, preventing him from attacking me. "I invited her here."

Sergei tore his eyes away from me and glared at Nic. "You brought a *human* to our home? To a lair filled with vampires? You must not think much of her then." His laughter echoed off the stone walls, making my skin crawl.

"I think more of her than I do you," Nic growled.

Sergei's eyes had a flash of red pass over them, his face scrunched. "Don't you ever talk to me like that again."

"Boys!" Henri jumped from his seat and put himself in between the two fighting vampires. "That's quite enough." He placed his hands on their chests and pushed them apart. I was impressed by his strength. He may have looked old and fragile, but he sure didn't act like it.

Henri turned to Sergei. "Now Sergei, you and I know Nic. He has shown us nothing but kindness, trust, and loyalty. He has been there for us when no one else has. He's protected us from the humans who wish us harm or even death. So I'm sure he had a very good reason for bringing her here. I trust her," he said, looking over at me and smiling. A grateful sigh left my body.

"But—"

"No, Sergei," Henri cut him off. "There is no room for discussion. Honoria will stay here, as long as she likes. And you will not give her any trouble. Do I make myself clear?"

The two stared at each other for a minute before Sergei finally backed off. He gave Henri a slight nod before turning and stalking off down a random hallway.

"I'm sorry for that, dear. Sergei has quite the temper at times. But he doesn't truly mean any of it."

I nodded. "He acted like that the first time I met him."

"Oh, you've met before?"

"Yes. It was not a pleasant experience. He, uh…" My voice broke off.

Nic cleared his throat. "He actually threatened to kill her."

Henri's eyes grew wide. "Oh, dear. Well, we will have to keep him away from you. But if you will excuse me, you two, it's been quite an evening. I think I'll turn in."

"Of course," I told him. "Thank you so much. For sticking up for me, and for telling me your story. I really appreciate it."

"Anytime, dear. I will see you tomorrow. And Nic, you take care of her." He winked.

"You got it."

"So." I cleared my throat, the sound echoing off the walls. "Besides Henri, I take it you're kind of, like, the head vampire around here?"

"I don't know about that. But they do tend to listen to me and show me some respect. And it's not like I boss them around or anything. Or send them off on mindless errands. But I do keep them in line. We have to have some sort of order around here." He shook his head then, turning to me. "Shall we continue on with the tour?"

CHAPTER ELEVEN

Honoria

"Why do you live underground?" I asked, genuinely curious. Normally, when you heard about vampires in books or movies, they would live in gorgeous Victorian houses, or go to high school as a senior for the millionth time, just trying to blend in.

Nic then explained, "We belong to the darkness. We're not ashamed of who we are. Why should we be?"

I stayed silent, not really having an answer to his question. If it was even a question to begin with.

Nic continued, "Besides, pretending to be a teenager, attending classes and 'graduating' year after year," he said with disgust in his voice, "gets tiring. Old. No one wants to do that forever. We're old souls, stuck inside a teenage-looking body. Well, most of us," he whispered, nodding back to where Henri had been sitting. I stifled my laughter, but with vampires having super hearing, I was pretty sure he heard me.

"And the reason most of us are stuck in teen form is because, well, that's the age when we go off on our own, isn't it?" he shrugged. "As children we need our parents, their help and their guidance. As we get older and into our teen years, we begin to gain some independence, trying to learn our way in this crazy world."

Makes sense. He answered a lot of my unasked questions.

"Down here we don't have to live a life of fear. We never have to worry about the sun, humans threatening us, or anything like that. It's more … peaceful. And if one of us should slip up and begin to speak in an old tongue, an ancient language, no one bats an eye. It happens way more often than you'd think," he said with a chuckle. "Maintaining the illusion we're only mere teenagers when truthfully we are scholars, world travelers, seekers of ancient knowledge is utterly exhausting. Too much work to please those who wish us dead." He balled his hands up into tight fists.

I felt bad. Even though I wasn't one who wished the vampires were wiped out, I was still human. So, I was a part of their anger, to a degree.

It wasn't fair.

"What's this?" I asked, running my hands along

what looked like a semi-hidden door in the wall. It felt warm, unlike every other inch of this place.

Nic stiffened beside me. "That's nothing," he uttered quickly, continuing down the hall. "Let's move on."

Strange. I wanted to know more, but I let it go for now and followed him. He showed me where each of the other vampires called home, the many common areas, and finally, we came to what would be my room.

"Here we are," he announced. He opened the door and I let out a gasp. It was nothing like I imagined. The rest of this place looked … well, like a tomb. But this room looked normal, like it belonged in a regular old house. "I hope you like it. I, um, I picked everything out myself. And Selene helped me put the room together. She's better at this sort of thing."

"You knew I'd be coming to stay?" I asked, eyebrows raised.

I had no idea if vampires were able to blush or not, with the lack of blood running through their veins, but I could swear I saw Nic blush.

"No, but I was hoping," he admitted. "I thought it would be nice to get things all set up and ready, just in case. Selene was overly excited. Both because we've never had a human down here before, and because she loved the idea of having another girl around."

I didn't think about the lack of women here.

"More men than women choose to become vampires," he said, reading my mind again. "Not that there aren't plenty of female vampires. There just tends to be more men, that's all." He shrugged.

"Well, I will leave you to it," he said. "Everything in this room is yours, so feel free to look around. And if you go out exploring, just be careful please."

I nodded. "Hey, Nic." I caught his arm just before he left. "Thank you. I can't tell you how much I appreciate everything you have done for me." I'd hate to think about what would have happened if it weren't for him. "You saved me, really. And I can't thank you enough."

His smile made my heart melt. "You're welcome, Honoria. You've had a hell of a few days. You should try and get some rest. If you need me, I'm just in the next room." The thought of Nic on the other side of the wall from me made me feel both nervous and comforted at the same time. Especially with Sergei roaming around the place. I just hoped his roaming wouldn't bring him into my room. I didn't have the strength to deal with him anymore tonight.

Once I was alone, I looked around at my new accommodations. For being a room underneath a mausoleum, it didn't look all that bad. Like the rest of the place, at least the areas I saw, it had the same color scheme—a lot of red and black, with a tiny bit of purple thrown in here and there. The large stone fireplace was lit, illuminating the room while making it feel warm and cozy. Well, as cozy as you could get underground in a cemetery. The four-poster bed was covered with a silky red comforter and sheets. A sheer, black material hung draped over the four vertical columns that were carved into intricate patterns. *How romantic.*

Along with the fireplace, lit black candles were scattered everywhere. The wax dripped down red, making them look like they were bleeding. I laughed at the sight of them—Vampires Tears candles were very popular around Halloween time. At least they seemed to have a sense of humor.

An antique looking dresser with matching vanity sat along the wall opposite the door. I walked over to it and ran my hands along the surprisingly smooth wood. Mother would have loved these. I could see her sitting in front of the mirror each morning, doing her hair and makeup. She aimed to look her best for Father, even though he thought she looked beautiful without a stitch of makeup on.

I hoped to find a love like theirs someday.

Picking up my bags, I put everything away and got settled in my temporary new home. I didn't know how long I would be here. Or how long I would be welcome here. I'm sure Sergei was already working on a plan to get me kicked out.

CHAPTER TWELVE

Nic

"What the hell were you thinking, bringing her here?" Sergei yelled as he burst in my room later on. He slammed the door shut so hard, I was afraid it would splinter. "After you lectured us about partying up in the cemetery and messing with humans," he scoffed. "You go ahead and bring one to live with us. How could you do that?!"

I let out a frustrated sigh. "I know what I said, Sergei. But this is entirely different."

"Of course it is." He threw his hands up in the air. "Because the almighty Nic wants it, huh. Who cares what others want, right?" he screamed right in my face.

"No," I began, trying to keep my voice even. "What you did was reckless and dangerous and you risked exposing us."

He shook his head in anger and started to walk away from me.

I wanted to let him leave for I didn't appreciate the accusations and screaming. But I also wanted to tell my side of things. "You know I'm extra careful when I go out among the human population," I continued. "When I go out, no one suspects a thing. I blend in. Unlike you," I pointed my finger in his face, "who is loud and loves to be seen. You torture humans for the fun of it."

I waited but he didn't deny it.

"And you are going to leave Honoria alone. Do you hear me?"

"Yes, master," he mocked.

I closed my eyes, taking a deep breath and pinching the bridge of my nose. I hated how he got to me like this. He was one of us, so of course I put up with him, but it was utterly exhausting. It was like caring for a thousand-year-old child.

"Just please, don't do anything to her," I pleaded, lowering my voice.

"But why?" he asked again. "Why did you bring her here?"

"I like her." I shrugged. What more was there to say? But then again, this was Sergei I was talking to. He wasn't going to just let this go. I didn't feel comfortable though telling him how I had this strong desire to be around her and this fierce need to protect her. It was absolutely none of this business.

"Like her?" Sergei scoffed. "You've only known her for two minutes."

"Sometimes, that's all you need," I spat back. Which was the truth. Sometimes when you know, you know.

Sergei stopped, eyebrows raised in amusement. "Man, I feel sorry for the women you date then."

"Shut it, Sergei. That's not what I meant and you know it."

He threw his hands up in the air. "Whatever you say, man."

I huffed out a small laugh. "So, are we okay then? She stays?"

"She stays," he finally agreed. He walked to the door, then stopped, hand on the door handle, "And I'm sorry for the outburst."

"No worries, man."

Once Sergei was gone, I sat in my leather armchair next to the fireplace, staring at the flames as they danced around.

I really hoped I was doing the right thing.

CHAPTER THIRTEEN

Honoria

My eyes burned with the need to sleep, but it wasn't coming easily. After tossing and turning for what seemed like hours, I finally decided to drag my butt out of bed and go exploring on my own a little. I didn't know what I expected to find, but I was curious to see how these vampires lived. Plus, I never could sleep easily in a new place. I'd been that way forever.

I found nothing too interesting on my little adventure. A lot of cold, dark hallways, and plenty of other rooms, which led me to wonder just how many vampires were down here. My mind kept wandering back to the mystery door Nic had been so weird about. He had to be hiding something big. Not just him, but all of the vampires. I knew I had to respect their rules, I was a guest in their home after all, but all I wanted to do was go find that door and open it up. It was so hard not to.

Along most of the hallways sat a few wooden benches, all old and worn but sturdy looking. They were probably put there for poor old Henri. He was such a sweet old vampire. Taking a seat, I leaned my head back against the cool stone wall as everything from the past few days came rushing back. The weight of my recent loss settled heavily on my shoulders. I couldn't hold back the tears any longer and they spilled over, flooding down my cheeks.

The sobs that accompanied them were so loud, I didn't hear Nic come up beside me, gently taking a seat next to me. I looked at him, eyes burning from crying, and sniffled. I felt so gross but he didn't say anything, silently putting his arms around me and pulling me to him. I leaned into his chest, welcoming his comforting touch. The only thing that threw me was his lack of a heartbeat. I had noticed it before and thought I was going crazy, but now I understood. Vampires weren't technically living, so they didn't have a heartbeat.

Nic said nothing for the longest time, letting me take my time and cry it out. This seemed to be a pattern with us. I would cry and Nic would come to the rescue. I really needed to get it together.

"Thank you," I said, sitting up and wiping my nose on the back of my hand. "I'm sorry we're always meeting like this." I laughed awkwardly, trying to lighten the mood.

"Hey, it's all right," Nic assured me. "You have every right to cry and be emotional. This is a tough time for you. A lot of things are changing in such a short time. You're only human." He smirked.

"True. But I should be such a …"

"Such a girl?" he offered, earning himself a light smack on the arm. He held his hands up in defeat. "I'm sorry. I'm sorry."

"You better be."

"So what's got you down?" Nic shifted on the bench, turning his body and attention towards me.

I faced him, eyebrows raised. "You sure you wanna hear all about my problems still? They seem to be never ending."

"True," he said slowly, raising his hands in the air, "but I've got nothing but time. Plus," he bumped my shoulder with his, "I care about your problems. I care about you."

Warmth spread throughout my body. Having someone care for me the way Nic did was completely new to me. It wasn't an unwelcome feeling, just new. Nothing I was used to.

But I wanted it to be familiar—an emotion I recognized.

"Are you missing your family?" he asked, when I hadn't answered his question. His voice was soft, and his concern was genuine and sweet.

"No." I shook my head. "I have no family left."

He raised an eyebrow at that. None at all?"

"Not that I know of," I confessed. "That's why I came back. When my parents passed," I added. "There was no one else. I waited a few days to begin planning the funeral, in case others showed up and wanted to help. I'm no good at this sort of thing," I said softly.

"Planning a funeral?"

"Saying goodbye." I avoided his eyes. We sat in silence again for a few minutes, neither of us knowing what to say. But I welcomed the silence. Right then, it was what I needed. Nic's presence next to me was enough.

My family and I were never really all that close. It was hard for me to let anyone in. How was I supposed to let go of the only two people in the world that meant even the slightest bit to me? The only people I had let in, even if not all the way. They were always there for me, no matter how awful I may have treated them. They always seemed to understand, even when I pushed them away.

And now, they were gone. And I was alone.

Having read my mind again, Nic moved closer, brushing up against me, letting me know he was here still. Just the slightest touch from him was comforting. He knew when to talk and when I needed silence, and I loved that about him.

I let out the breath I had been holding. "I think I'm fine now," I said, only half-lying. I knew Nic would know if I was or not, but I didn't want to become a huge burden to him. Not any more than I already was. And this whole whiney, crying all the time, damsel in distress thing wasn't me. I hated feeling this way.

"You sure?"

I nodded, not trusting myself to speak. Nic looked me over, but didn't say anything.

"Do you need help finding your way back? I know this place can seem like a maze."

"I think I can manage," I answered. "But hey," I grabbed his arm, "thank you. Again." I rolled my eyes. "I know you're probably sick of having to play knight in shining armor with me all the time."

"Nonsense." He shook his head. "I don't mind at all. I just want to make sure you're okay." He gave me that heart-stopping smile.

I looked down at my feet. "Well, I appreciate it. More than you know," I added, my voice barely above a whisper.

"Anytime." Leaning over, he planted a kiss on my forehead. "You really should go get some rest though."

I nodded again just as he turned to retreat to his room. As I navigated the labyrinth on my own, I ran into two more vampires, lost in conversation. I didn't know whether to turn and walk back the way I'd come or just continue on past them. I hadn't met everyone yet and didn't know if these two would be friendly, or like Sergei.

"Oh, hi!" the female said, her voice bubbly and light.

She and her companion started walking towards me. "You must the human!" she exclaimed, sniffing the air.

I tried not to show just how uncomfortable that made me. "I am, yes." My eyes darted around, searching for an escape plan just in case.

"Oh, welcome to our home!" The woman bounced over and pulled me into a hug, crushing me with her vampire strength. I'd never get used to just how strong they were.

"I'm Selene," she said, releasing me from her strong grip. "Selene Michaels. And this," she turned to the shy vampire behind her, "is Cody Stevens." Cody offered a small wave.

I relaxed a little. These two seemed friendly enough. "Nice to meet you," I said. "I'm Honoria Prescott."

"We've heard so much about you," Selene said, bright blonde hair bouncing along with her. She had so much energy, I had no idea how I would ever keep up with her.

"You have?"

"Of course! Nic would not shut up about you. Not that that's a bad thing," she quickly added. "He just seems to really like you. And I mean *really* like you," she teased.

"It's true," Cody added with a sly smile. "You're all he seems to talk about lately."

I couldn't decide if that was a good thing or a bad thing.

"Sergei either, but that's an entirely different story."

Selene rolled her eyes. "Not that you have anything to worry about," she added quickly. "He won't be a problem. We'll see to that." She nodded to Cody, who smiled back in agreement.

"I am sorry to hear about your parents," Cody said, coming close to me. He looked like he was about to hug me, but opted to just rub a comforting hand up and down my arm instead.

"It must be so awful. I can't even imagine," Selene didn't hesitate to pull me in for another hug. Boy was she friendly.

"Thank you," I answered quietly. "It's … difficult."

"I bet, poor thing. Well, if you ever need anything we're both here for you. Anytime."

I looked at them both and smiled. "Thank you. Again." I let out a small laugh. I didn't know what I expected when meeting so many vampires, but I never imagined they would be so caring and friendly. More so than any human I'd ever met. Besides my parents, that is.

Once I was alone again, I decided to go check out that strange wooden door. If Nic hadn't acted the way he did, I probably would have left it alone.

It looked like any other door to me. I glanced right and left, making sure I was alone before trying the handle.

Locked. I tried harder, but the dang thing wouldn't budge.

I pressed my ear up to the door, hoping to hear

something from the inside that would give me a hint as to what lay on the other side. But no matter how hard I strained, I couldn't hear a single sound. It left me more frustrated than before. I needed to know what lay on the opposite side.

"Are you supposed to be sneaking around there?' Sergei's voice startled me.

Slowly, I turned to face him, heat creeping up the back of my neck. I put on my best innocent look. "I'm not sneaking," I said, trying to keep my voice from giving away just how nervous I really was being alone with him in a dark hallway.

"Uh, huh. Sure," he said, stepping close to me—so much I could feel the heat coming off his body. He must have fed recently. "You can calm down," he told me after about a full minute of silence. "I'm not going to hurt you."

"I'm fine." I shook my head.

"I can hear your heartbeat. It's going a mile a minute. I promise you, I won't touch you." He backed up a step to show he was telling the truth.

I tried to calm my nerves, but Sergei seemed unpredictable. Plus, he did want to kill me the first time we met.

But then his expression changed and a smirk spread across his face. "Unless you really aren't scared of me, and it's something else entirely." He winked. "I do have that effect on women."

"Are you always this arrogant and cocky?" I asked him, all nervousness leaving my body.

He stepped closer to me again with a wicked smile on his face. "Do you wanna find out?" he asked suggestively.

Gross. "Not in a million years." I pushed him away.

"We can arrange that."

I shot him a look, unsure of what he meant. Then it hit me—I could become a vampire. He wouldn't do that to me against my will, would he? I knew he had questionable morals, but would he really sink that low? The thought absolutely terrified me. I snuck a look at Sergei out the corner of my eye. He gave me a reassuring smile, while backing up and raising both hands in surrender.

Right, the vampire mind-reading thing.

I took in a few deep breaths, feeling a little better.

"Well, I think you have had enough excitement for the day." Sergei let out an uncomfortable laugh. "I'll let you be on your way. I'm sorry to have disturbed you."

I agreed with him there. "Thank you," I nodded. "Goodnight."

CHAPTER FOURTEEN

Honoria

"Hey, Nic," I said softly as I knocked on his bedroom door, "would it be all right if I left for a bit?"

He set down the ancient looking journal he had been looking at and motioned for me to come inside. His room looked quite similar to mine, only it was three times the size, at least. He had not one, but two fireplaces which were both lit, making the cavernous room feel cozy.

"I don't see why not," he answered.

I nodded. "Okay. I just wasn't sure if I would be allowed to come and go. Or if I'd be allowed back in if I left. I know how Sergei feels about me being here," my voice grew quiet.

"Don't worry about him," Nic shook his head. "Sergei won't bother you. But where are you heading?" he asked, getting up to place the journal on one of the many shelves that lined his walls.

I shifted on my feet. "Back to my old apartment."

Nic stopped what he was doing and looked my way, worry etched on his face. "You're leaving?"

"Just for a few hours. At the most," I answered quickly. I guessed I could have worded that better. The worry eased off his face, replaced with relief.

"Well, good."

"I just left some stuff back at my old apartment and figured I should bring it here. Or at least to my parents' place." I didn't think I'd ever get out of the habit of calling it their house. Even if I fully moved in there, it would always be theirs to me.

"You're not going back there?"

I shook my head. "With everything that's happened, I don't think I could."

"Understandable." Nic set the book on the shelf and walked over to me. "Would you like some company? I could come with you and help pack up your belongings if you'd like."

The thought of being alone with Nic for any amount of time made me nervous. But I could really use the help. "Thank you," I said. "I'd love that."

· · ·

The car ride was a silent one. I was anxious enough as it was bringing a vampire to meet my old friends. Nic would no doubt be on his best behavior, but what if they suspected anything? And worse—what if Dylan showed up? I would be happy to never have to see or deal with him again.

"We're here," I announced, pulling the car into the parking garage. Besides my glamorous job as a checkout girl at the local grocery store, I attended college full time. I had been lucky enough to find an apartment in the middle of the city. My roommates, Anna and Tracy, were the most energetic, loud, loving people you'd ever meet. They welcomed me with open arms and quickly wanted to become my best friends.

They both reminded me of Selene. She would have loved them and gotten along with both of them perfectly. For a second, I wished I had brought her instead of Nic, but then again, I just wanted to get my stuff and get out.

We stopped in front of the door to my apartment. "You ready for this?" I asked, sticking my key in the lock. I should warn you, Abby and Tracy are both a little … much. It's like two more Selenes running around." I laughed.

"I think I can handle it." Nic smiled back.

I turned the key and opened the door. The place looked the same as when I'd left a few weeks ago.

Had it really been that long already? It seemed like just yesterday I got the call about my parents.

"Honoria?" Tracy's voice broke through my thoughts. "Is that you?"

"It's me," I answered.

She rushed over and pulled me into a hug, crushing my bones. "I have been so worried about you! You never called," she said, pushing me back a bit so she could look me in the eyes. "*We* were so worried about you."

"I'm sorry." I felt horrible. I could have at least picked up the phone to call, or shoot off a text telling them I was all right. "I had a lot going on." I knew it sounded like just another excuse, but it was true. I had so much on my mind, most of which I couldn't tell her.

She waved off my answer. "It's okay. Your parents passing … it's a lot to deal with."

"It was. Still is." I nodded. "Where's Abby?"

Tracy looked over her shoulder towards Abby's room, which was situated in the middle of her and my room. "She has classes all day. I have a break for about another hour. So how are you feeling? And better yet, who is the hunk you brought with you?" She turned all her attention to Nic, who was standing awkwardly by the door. I forgot to also warn him that Tracy was absolutely boy-crazy.

"This is Nic, my uh …"

"Friend from back home, in Glenfall Heights," he finished for me.

"Yea, we go way back," I lied.

Tracy walked over to him. "You've never mentioned

him before." She held out her hand. "I'm Tracy Brooks." She smiled seductively at him. My insides clenched with jealousy.

Nic grabbed her hand lightly. "Nic Blackwood. It's a pleasure to meet you."

With the look she had on her face, I thought Tracy was going to melt into a puddle right then and there.

"The pleasure is all mine," she purred.

"Anyway," I interrupted whatever was going on between the two of them, "I just came to get my stuff."

Tracy snapped out of her trance. "Wait? You're moving out."

"I am. I should have given you more warning. I'm sorry."

"A little heads up would have been nice, but I get it. You need to be back home at a time like this. But I am sure gonna miss you."

I pulled her into a quick hug. "I'm going to miss you too, Tracy. We've made some wonderful memories here."

Tracy wiped a tear from her eye. "I just wish Abby was here to say goodbye."

"I know. But I promise I'll call her. I'll keep in touch with you both."

"You better," she said, hauling some boxes and suitcases out of the hall closet. "I kept these when we all moved in, so we would have them for the move out." She shrugged.

"Smart," Nic told her. I could see her cheeks turning a lovely shade of red.

"Thank you. I'll help take this to your room. Do you need help packing?"

"Sure, if you don't mind."

"Not at all." She looked Nic up and down. I made a mental note to never leave her alone with him.

Despite offering, Tracy didn't actually help with any of the packing. Instead, she plopped herself down on my old bed and struck up conversation with Nic. I didn't mind too much for it gave me time to sort through my belongings and pack the ones I actually wanted.

"Oh!" Tracy yelled, startling me. I dropped the stack of books I was carrying. "Sorry." She scrunched her face. "I just remembered, Dylan stopped by a few days ago."

I stopped halfway to picking the books back up. "Seriously?"

"He sure did. He was all pissed off about something. We didn't let him in though. What happened between you two anyway?"

I looked over at Nic. "I just got sick of the way he was treating me." Which wasn't a lie. I just should have broken up with him sooner. "I ended things and he went all psycho. Luckily, Nic was there to save the day." I smiled sweetly at him. A flash of something crossed Tracy's eyes. Resentment? Jealousy?

"A regular knight in shining armor, huh?" she teased. "But good for you. I never liked Dylan."

"Wish you would have told me sooner." I laughed, then put the books in the box. "All done," I announced.

"Well, we weren't much help at all, huh?" Nic said with a grin.

I shook my head. "Nope, but it's all right. I didn't have too much to pack. Tracy, I left those for you," I nodded towards the stack of neatly folded shirts on the end of the bed. "I know you've been eyeing them. So they're yours."

She got up and checked them out. "Thank you so much. I do love them," she admitted.

The two of them helped lug all my belongings to the car. Nic got in the driver's seat and I turned to Tracy. "Thank you for everything. You were such a great friend. I'll miss you."

She pulled me into another bone-crushing hug. "I'm gonna miss you, too. And we can always come visit or you can come back here. This isn't forever."

"Absolutely," I lied. As much as I loved her and Abby, I couldn't see myself getting together with them for girly nights out on the town. It had never been my thing.

Selene and Cody were sitting on the couch in my bedroom when Nic and I arrived back at the lair with my stuff. "Welcome back!" she declared as Cody moved to help with the rest of the boxes.

"Is that everything?" he asked.

"Yup," I stared down at the pile on the floor. "I am officially all moved in."

"Well, not until you unpack," Selene pointed out.

"True."

"Do you need help with that or …" Nic asked.

I shook my head. "You've done more than enough today. Thank you, I really appreciate it."

Nic grinned and bowed, sweeping his hand out to the side. "Anytime."

***

"Girl, tell us everything," Selene said as she shut the door behind Nic.

"What is there to tell?" I asked honestly. All we did was pack up my crap while my old roommate flirted with Nic right in front of me. Selene would have a field day with that information.

"All right," she said slowly. "So what about you and Nic? What's going on there?" She wiggled her eyebrows at me.

"What do you mean?"

"Oh, come on," she insisted. "There's something going on between the two of you, even if you don't see it."

The back of my neck felt like it was on fire. I looked

to Cody for help but he just gave me a knowing smile and shook his head. "I don't know what you're talking about."

"Sure." She rolled her eyes. "You and Nic are made for each other, plain and simple," she stated. "Everyone can see it."

Cody chimed in. "It's true. I don't know much about love or relationships in general, but there's something powerful between you two.

Selene was bouncing in her seat excitedly. "You would make the most perfect couple. And I would totally support it happening."

"Me too," Cody agreed.

I would be lying if I said I hadn't thought about it. I don't know if it was because we had spent so much time together or because he was always rescuing me at every turn, but I did feel something for Nic. "I don't even think he likes me that way," I said sheepishly.

"That's a lie and you know it, girl." Selene rolled her eyes. "You two were totally meant for each other. You know it, I know it. Hell, I'm sure even Sergei knows it."

My turn to roll my eyes. "Please don't mention any of this to Sergei."

"Fine, I won't tell him you guys are totally in love," she teased, bending down to grab a suitcase. "Anyway, we came to help you get settled in." She nodded towards Cody.

We spent the next few hours unpacking my things and gossiping. I truly felt at home here now.

Once everything was put away and those two headed off to bed, I looked around the room, which was now filled with everything I owned. The lump in my throat dissolved into tears, and they freely fell down my face in waves.

My whole life was changing, and nothing would ever be the same again.

CHAPTER FIFTEEN

Honoria

"So how are you adjusting to life in the crypt, as I call it?" Selene asked me. She and Cody had been stopping by my room to hang out pretty much every day. At first, the constant intrusion annoyed me but I quickly grew to love their visits. It was nice not to have to be alone.

My shoulders bobbed up and down. "It's fine."

"Really?" Cody eyed me.

"Really. I mean, it was a lot to take in and get used to at first," I admitted, "but I feel I've gotten pretty settled in by now. And Sergei has finally started to leave me alone." It took him a couple weeks to lay off me, but he did.

Selene leaned back against my bed. We were all

seated on the floor, which was what we did whenever we gossiped. I had a rug so fluffy and thick, it was like sitting on a cloud. "That's true. I have noticed he's not as much of a jerk as he usually is."

Cody nodded in agreement. "He's even stopped calling me names."

"He calls you names?"

"Yea, well, one name. But I hate it." He clenched both his fists. "He'd started calling me Baby Blood," he seethed.

I wrinkled my nose. "Baby Blood?"

"Instead of Bloodling." He shook his head.

Selene scooted closer to him on the rug and laid her head on his shoulder, rubbing his arms. Cody unclenched his fists and his expression softened. I smiled, watching those two. I wondered why they'd never confessed their feelings for each other. I could clearly see the love that sparked between them.

Selene's eyes lit up. "Hey! Isn't the town Halloween party soon?" she asked.

I had to stop and think about what day it was. "Yeah, tomorrow I think."

"Do you think we would be able to go?" She gestured to the three of u, then stood and jumped on the balls of her feet, her excitement building with each second. "I've always wanted to go, but Nic would never let me." As she said Nic's name, she rolled her eyes and made a face.

"He says it's too dangerous," Cody said to Selena, causing her to huff.

She turned to face him. "I know what he says. But now we have her." She pointed her thumb back towards me. "The entire town knows Honoria," she explained when Cody raised his eyebrows in question. "They know she's normal. Human. They wouldn't bat an eye at us if we were with her."

"That's true," Cody admitted. "Do you really think he'd go for it?"

Selene shrugged, her blonde hair bouncing up and down with her shoulders. "Couldn't hurt to ask. What do you think?" Both vampires turned their attention towards me.

To spending the evening out at a party with two new-ish vampires. In the town square filled with humans. What could go wrong?

"I guess there's no harm in asking." I usually avoided any town party or gathering of any kind. But Selene and Cody were both so darn excited. I didn't have the heart to tell them that I'd rather stay home, and ruin their fun.

It was only one night. I'd survive.

Right?

Selene clapped her hands together with excitement. "Yay! Oh, thank you," she squeaked, running to give me a hug. We almost toppled over, with Selene and her vampire strength.

"Let's go find Nic." She beamed.

It took a bit of convincing and multiple promises that we would be extra careful, but Nic finally agreed to let us go.

"Please, I am begging you, keep an eye on those two. At all times," he whispered, pulling me aside.

"Aren't they old enough to take care of themselves?" I asked, raising my eyebrows.

"They are, technically. But they're still Bloodlings," he pointed out. "Especially Cody. Those two are still learning and," he dropped his voice even lower," I'm not one hundred percent sure they have their cravings completely under control."

I nodded slowly. "Got it. I promise, we won't get into any trouble."

"Thanks," he said with a smile. "I'm counting on you."

Great, not only did I have to attend a huge party I didn't really want to go to, but I was solely responsible for two Bloodlings. Hopefully, they wouldn't be in the mood to snack on the town.

The party was worse than I imagined. It seemed every single person in town had showed up. Most wore a costume, Selene included. She chose a mini ruffled skirt with a matching shirt, witch hat and broom.

She'd tried, but failed to get both Cody and me into a costume. He'd instead thrown on an orange sweater over jet black jeans while Selene had loaned me one of her dresses. It was black, with the bottom of the skirt looking like a foggy night with stars and a bright white moon. It came up just above my knees, and I actually really loved it.

The town square was decked out in orange, black, purple and green. Fake spider webs and twinkly lights hung from the trees. Couples were seated on hay bales set up near the food and drink stalls.

Children's laughter rang out from the many game booths, the pumpkin carving stations, and the myriad rides scattered throughout the square.

"What should we do first?" Selene asked as we walked past someone bobbing for apples in a huge black plastic cauldron. I hadn't done that in years.

"Definitely not that." I eyed the dance floor covered with fog that changed colors as the lights pulsed with the music.

Selene laughed.

"How about a snack?" Cody suggested.

I stopped in my tracks, heart pounding. I looked over at him, eyes wide.

"Not what I meant." He pointed to the rows of caramel apples, orange-colored cotton candy, and the orange, purple, and green snow cones. He shook his head and laughed, as I let out a huge sigh.

"I'm sorry, guys. I guess I'm a little on edge. This is so new for me."

Selene nudged me. "Having vampires as friends?"

"Yeah, that." I laughed.

"Don't worry, we'll be on our best behavior."

"As far as anyone knows, we're human tonight," Cody added with a wink.

I felt embarrassed for not trusting them. They'd lived here for this long undetected. They weren't about to do something stupid.

"I know, thank you," I added, accepting the cotton candy Selene handed me. Another thing I hadn't had in forever. Maybe the sticky sugar would help calm my nerves.

Selene was the most excited out of the three of us to be here. Cody and I followed her and she bounced from booth to booth, throwing darts at balloons and trying to knock over heavy glass bottles. I didn't care too much to participate and Cody seemed like he was just really enjoying her company.

They finally convinced me to try out a game. We chose basketball, since it had three nets and we could all play at the same time. I was setting up my next shot when piercing screams rang throughout the air. Dropping my ball, I whipped around, searching for the source of the screaming.

"Over there!" Cody pointed and we took off running. A few others were also racing towards the screams, but most went in the opposite direction. Part of me wanted to go with them.

Right in the center of the town square was complete chaos. Blood, ripped clothing, and what looked like a hand were strewn about.

"Oh, my god," Selene whispered.

"What?" I whispered back, feeling sick.

She nodded to the gruesome scene ahead of us. "There are real vampires among them."

My eyes grew wide. "Seriously?"

Selene nodded.

"How could you tell?" I looked around, a few people running by us were dressed up in vampire costumes. I couldn't tell a real one from a fake.

"They're kind of the ones biting people in the necks and ripping their limbs off," Cody said without a hint of humor in his voice.

I fought back a fresh wave of nausea.

"Just stay behind us."

"Stay hidden," Selene added, pushing me towards the gazebo with decorated hay bales stacked in it. The two of them ran into the chaos without a second thought. The newer vampires dropped their victims, snarling. As hard as I tried, my human eyes couldn't keep up with their vampire speed. The entire fight looked like nothing more than a blur to me. One had Cody by the throat, lifting him off the ground. Another rushed at Selene, but she held her own, kicking the vampire in the chest so hard, he actually flew into the air, hitting his back against a tree and slumping to the ground. He got back up in a flash, ran straight at her, and clotheslined her. She fell hard, hitting her head with a sickening crack.

Cody, the vampire's hands still wrapped around his throat, looked positively pissed. "A little help over here, Selene?" She rushed to his aid, throwing them both to the ground. "What do you want?" she asked the vampire. "What are you doing here?" He tried to run but they held him firmly in place.

"I don't have to answer you," he spat.

"Nunzio, let's go. We've gotta get out of here," his friend said, sounding a little nervous. "Dario never said anything about other vampires."

Dario? Who the hell was that? Or what?

Nunzio used this distraction as an opportunity to wriggle out of Selene's grasp, and he and his mystery friend took off in a blur.

"What the hell was that?" I asked, crawling out of my hiding spot. I felt so useless and ashamed. I should have helped them but I didn't lift a finger. I hid. Like a coward.

"No idea," Cody said, rubbing his sore neck. "But let's get out of here as well."

"Are you sure you're okay?" Selene asked him, her voice dripping with concern.

He nodded. "I'm fine, just a little embarrassed. But thank you, Selene. I owe you. You saved my life."

She smiled, pulling him into a hug. "You owe me

nothing. You're my friend. And I know you would do the same for me." He wrapped his arms around her, and they held each other tight for a second. It was a simple gesture, yet so intimate I had to look away.

"Let's get going now." Selene looped her arm through mine, and we returned to our crypt.

CHAPTER SIXTEEN

Honoria

"**S**ee, this is exactly why I didn't want you guys to go in the first place!" Nic yelled, his voice echoing off the stone walls. "This is why we stay hidden, why we don't venture out and mingle with humans." He pointed to Cody and Selene, both covered in blood and their clothes torn. "What if Honoria had gotten hurt. Or worse—killed?" He let out a disappointed groan.

"This isn't fair! They did absolutely nothing wrong. And how were they to know that two rogue vampires would crash the Halloween party? Besides, nothing happened to me, Nic. I'm fine." I argued.

"Yeah, because you were hiding." Sergei chuckled from the corner.

"Why are you even here?" I turned to him. "Don't you have someone else to torture?"

"Not at all." Sergei shrugged. "Besides, you are my favorite person to torture. You just make it so easy."

I wanted to punch that smug look right off his face. "Just leave me alone."

He got right up in my face. "It's not my fault you're such a coward."

Irritation settled deep in my chest. I was so sick of dealing with jerks like him.

"That's enough, Sergei. You need to leave," Nic ordered. "*Now*," he said when he hadn't moved an inch. Sergei stared me directly in the eye for a long while before turning to leave.

I turned back to Nic, anger and shame coming off me in waves. "Sergei's right. I am a coward. And I wouldn't have to run and hide in a future attack if I was a vampire too."

The three of them sucked in a breath. "Do you want to become a vampire?" Selene asked. Until now, she and Cody had been silent as Nic berated us.

"I …" I didn't know how to answer that. *Did* I want to be a vampire? "I hadn't thought about it until now, honestly," I admitted. Which was the truth. Being a vampire was never something I had ever wanted. I never even imagined such a possibility before. Living with a bunch of them for a few weeks must be messing with my mind.

"Well, I think you would make an awesome

vampire," Selene gushed. "Besides, I think we could use more female vamps around here." She shrugged. Nic shot her a look. "What?" She shrugged. It's true and you know it. It's hard being the only female around here."

"Even so," he turned his attention back to me, making me nervous even though I'd done nothing wrong, "I don't think it would be a good idea."

"And why not?" I demanded. I put my hands on my hips, waiting for his answer.

"You're not strong enough. You're not in the right frame of mind to be making these kinds of decisions right now."

"Excuse me? Just what the hell do you mean by that?"

"She *is* strong, Nic," Cody said as Nic opened his mouth to say something. "And she's an adult. She can think for herself."

"It's her choice, Nic. Really," Selene added.

Nic held up his hand. "I think you two should go and get cleaned up. I need to talk to Honoria alone." Selene looked as if she was about to say something but closed her mouth and she and Cody headed off down the hall.

"What do you think you are doing?" he asked once they were out of earshot.

"I'm not doing anything, Nic."

"You're not thinking clearly, that's for sure."

"And you're being a jerk, that's for sure." I crossed my arms over my chest. "Nothing you said was fair.

Yeah, I hid during the attack. I panicked and didn't know what else to do. Selene told me to hide, so I did."

"You guys shouldn't have gone in the first place."

I scoffed. "Yeah, because we could have known there would be other vampires there." I shook my head angrily. " I thought you guys were the only ones in town."

"That's what I thought, too." He shook his head, his voice growing softer. "But that's not what we're talking about here. How could you say you want to be a vampire? You've been here for a short while; you've listened to our stories. We have such broken lives." He began to pace up and down the hallway. "Why would anyone ever choose to be like us? To live like this. On purpose?"

So I could be with you forever. That thought crept in out of nowhere. Nic and I barely knew each other, and here I was thinking about being with him forever? I shouldn't be thinking like this.

"I heard your stories, yes," I agreed. "But I heard nothing that would make me not want to become a vampire. Honestly, it doesn't sound that bad. Yes, forever is quite a long time," I said quickly, before he could interrupt me, "but if you have the right person by your side, it can't be that bad, right? I mean …" The way Nic was looking at me made my heart stop. "What?" I asked.

Instead of answering, he took a step towards me and pressed his lips to mine. With one hand around my waist, he pulled me closer to him while gently putting his other hand around the back of my head. The kiss was full of passion and hunger, like nothing I'd ever experienced before.

Nic paused, resting his forehead on mine. Our breaths came out ragged, and I found myself unable to speak.

"Are you okay?" he finally asked.

More than okay.

"I didn't mean to … I should have asked if you wanted it first. I'm sorry."

"No." I shook my head. I took his head in my hands. "You have absolutely nothing to be sorry about. I know you can read my mind. You're aware this was something I have been wanting to happen for a while now," I admitted. Heat traveled through me. But it felt good to finally tell him how I feel. It was like a huge weight being lifted off my chest.

Nic breathed out. "I will admit I have been wanting the same. Since before you came to stay down here."

"You have?"

He nodded. "There was a time back at your parents' house, when I was comforting you. It just felt right somehow. And I knew I wanted to be close to you. That I wanted you."

I was wracking my brain, trying to think of the exact moment he was talking about, but there were so many times he had been there for me, rescued me.

"That's the main reason why I am so opposed to you

becoming a vampire," he admitted. "I want to protect you, to keep you safe, always."

"But I also should be able to take care of myself," I argued. I moved down the hall to sit on one of the benches, Nic close behind. "When we met, I was a complete mess. You had to rescue me so many times, it's embarrassing."

"It's not embarrassing." He stroked down the side of my cheek with his thumb. His fingers left my skin hot wherever he touched.

"It really is. I was a total mess."

"You had good reason to."

"Still," I shifted my weight on the wooden bench.

Nic took my hands in his, and lowered his voice to a soothing tone, "No. You first lose your parents, both of them. Then you come back here, to a town you say you hate, and in the middle of all this, you lose your boyfriend and move away from the life you had made for yourself. That's an awful lot to deal with all at once. I think you did pretty well with it all, actually."

"I couldn't have made it through without you. I really couldn't. I would have completely fallen apart if it weren't for you. I'm not good with emotions or anything like that. I'm really not. So thank you, Nic. Thank you for saving me."

Nic leaned closer, planting a kiss on the top of my head. "Anytime. I will always be here to protect you." I leaned into him and closed my eyes, letting him comfort me. "Take tonight and think about it. Then maybe we can revisit the possibility of you becoming a vampire. Maybe."

Nic left to tend to some other vampire business. Pulling my knees to my chest, I thought about what he had said. I still had no clue where the idea of me turning had come from, but now it was all I could think about.

Someone dropping onto the bench beside me startled me out of my thoughts. "What are we pouting about today?"

I scoffed. "What do you want, Sergei?"

He held his hand over his heart, feigning offense. "Can't I just check on a friend without the third degree?"

"We're not friends," I pointed out. "Not even close."

"So mean," he shook his head. "Look, I'm sorry to have bothered you. I'll be on my way."

"Wait!" I grabbed him by the arm as he began to stand up. I knew I was going to regret this, but I wanted everyone's opinion. He stared at my hand on his arm and then looked at me, raising an eyebrow. "Sorry," I quickly let go of him.

He raised his hands in the air. "No harm done. Now, what did you need?"

I took a deep breath. "Please don't make me regret this, but I need your opinion on something important."

"Why not go to Nic? Don't you two have a little something going on between you?"

"One, I already did. And two, none of your business."

"All right. I'm just saying, you two have been looking a little cozy lately."

"Anyway," I shook my head, wanting to change the subject. This was the last thing I wanted to talk to Sergei about. "What would you think … about me becoming a vampire?" I squeezed my eyes shut, waiting for him to yell at me or something.

Instead, he took a seat again on the bench. "Well," he breathed out. "Is that what you truly want?"

I had been expecting him to be his usual self, all snarky and condescending. Not like this. "I hadn't thought about it at first, but the more I do, the more … yea, I do want it."

He was silent for a moment. "Honestly, I think it would be a great thing."

"Seriously?" I asked, a little shocked.

"Seriously. Look, I know I've been hard on you. But I'm that way with everyone. It's just who I am. Living for hundreds of years can do that to a person." He smirked.

I hadn't thought about that. But I guess it did make sense. I'm sure they'd all seen some horrible things in the time they'd walked this earth.

"You're not against it then?"

"Not at all." He shook his head, his dark brown hair swaying back and forth with the movement. "When you first showed up, I was angry."

"Very angry," I pointed out.

Sergei laughed. "Very angry, yes. Only because we had fought hard for so long to keep ourselves safe in this human world. Safe from humans," he clarified. "And without consulting any of us, Nic brought one here to live with us. So, I hope you can understand where I was coming from."

I shrank back in my seat. He was right. I just sort of barged in on their lives without so much as a warning. "I'm sorry."

"It's not your fault." He waved me off. "It was Nic. He listens to his heart way more than any creature of the night should. But, the more I got to know you, the more I learned about you. You're so much stronger than you let on. Tougher than you think. You were drowning in heartache when we met, but you managed to pull yourself out. I think you would make one badass vampire."

"Thank you." I smiled at him. It meant so much more coming from him. And somehow, this made me feel better about my decision. "For taking the time to talk with me."

"Anytime. Was there anything else?"

I shook my head.

"Good. But seriously," he turned to look me in the eye. "If you say anything to anyone about his conversation, not only will I deny it, but I'll have to kill you."

There's the Sergei I know.

"It's our little secret.'

Sergei nodded and, in a blur, he took off down the corridor.

Our conversation solidified the thoughts in my head. Now all that remained was to talk to Nic once more.

CHAPTER SEVENTEEN

Honoria

I waited a few more days to bring the idea back up to Nic. I took everything everyone had said into consideration. Once I made this decision, there was no going back.

Cody and Selene popped their heads into my room shortly after I had opened my eyes. "Oh, good. You're awake," Selene announced, coming into the room.

Cody followed closely behind her, his hands shoved deep in his pockets. "Morning."

"Morning, guys."

"So," Selene dragged out the word, crawling into bed beside me, "is today the day you're finally going to talk to Nic?"

She had been waiting for me to talk with him ever since I blurted out after the party that I might want to turn. She would find me and ask me about a thousand times a day if I had talked with him yet.

I nodded slowly, lobbing my gaze between my two best friends. "I am, yes."

She squealed and clapped her hands together. "Yay! It's about time, girl." She fluffed up the pillows and wiggled around, making herself more comfortable. "Ok, so now I have to ask, what exactly is going on between the two of you?" Her eyebrows wagged.

"What do you mean?" I asked, avoiding her gaze.

"Oh, don't give me that." She laughed. "We've seen the two of you together. You seem …" she seemed to search for the correct word, "… closer."

I should have known this was coming. Selene had been bugging me and teasing me since the day I let it slip out how I felt about him. We talked countless hours about it as well. Never about her and Cody though, although the sparks between them could be seen from space.

"You two promise not to tell anyone?" I asked, knowing damn well they wouldn't.

"Cross my heart."

I leaned in to her. "He kissed me."

Her mouth fell wide open. "No way. When was this?"

"Two nights ago."

"And you didn't rush over and let me know the second it happened?" She shot me an offended look.

"I'm sorry?" I offered, hoping that would be enough for her.

"Oh, it's all right." She threw her arms around me. "I'm just so happy you two are finally together."

Well, I didn't know about together-together. Nic and I hadn't talked about that either. After everything that had happened the other night, he had been giving me space to think over my decision.

"All right," I said before I lost my nerve. "Do you think you could get everyone to meet in the common area? I figured I would discuss this with everybody all at once, since my decision sort of affects you all, especially with me living here."

Cody nodded. "You got it." He smiled sweetly at Selene before heading out of the room.

"I'm so excited about this." Selene gathered me into a hug once more. "I have waited forever for another female vampire to walk these halls with me."

"I still have to get dressed though," I pointed out. I did not want to talk to everyone in my pajamas.

"Oh, yea. Okay, I'll go help Cody gather everyone and we'll meet you in the common room."

"Thank you," I said, throwing the covers back and walking over to my closet. I wondered what you would wear to tell a room full of vampires you want to become one of them.

I walked in to find all six vampires—Shade, Nic, Selene, Henri, Cody, and Sergei—sitting around the empty fireplace, staring at me in anticipation. That did nothing to calm my nerves.

I cleared my throat, the sound of it echoing off the stone walls. After taking in a shaky breath, I decided to just get on with it, especially since I already seemed to have everyone's attention.

"I'm guessing you guys already know why I asked you to meet with me," I said slowly. Selene had an excited look on her face already, Henri and Cody nodded, and Sergei looked like he'd rather be anywhere but here. Which was probably true. Shade was, true to his name, sitting back in the shadows, looking neither bored nor excited, while Nic smiled encouragingly at me.

"I have given this a lot of thought," I continued, "so I'm not just making a spur of the moment decision here. But," I looked each vampire in the eye briefly, "I want to become a vampire."

Murmuring and whispers ensued, while Selene predictably jumped up and squealed.

"It's not just because of my time spent with you, although that was a major factor." I snuck a glance at Nic. "I have been fascinated by vampires my entire life. Always hoping they were real and wishing to someday see one."

"And now, I have met some amazing vampires." I gestured to my new friends. "I have heard your stories, both good and bad. I know you all have done some horrible things in your lifetime. But that doesn't make you a bad person. Or vampire," I added when I caught Sergei rolling his eyes. "But this is what I want."

Nic stood from where he was perched on the arm of the worn-out sofa. "And you are absolutely sure about this?"

"Yeah," I answered him easily.

"You do realize what you would be giving up?" he asked, pacing back and forth now. What was he doing? Why was he questioning my decision? Didn't he want us to be together? It wasn't something I could exactly ask him in front of everyone. Especially since I didn't know what was going on between us. But we would have that talk tonight, I decided.

"We belong to the shadows," Nic continued when I didn't answer him. "And vampires, for the most part, have no real regard for human life. We love inflicting pain and torture on humans. Some more than others." He glanced at Sergei, who met his gaze with a shrug. He looked so smug. I thought back to the first night I had met him in the graveyard. Sergei had certainly seemed like he was having the time of his life while torturing me.

I shook my head. "What are you doing, Nic? You know I have loved everything there is about vampires. We talked about it the first night you told me what you were. You sat in my bedroom as we talked about this. Do you really not remember?"

Sergei made some rude comments I preferred to pretend not to hear.

"Nothing happened," I grumbled. "We only talked."

He put up his hands in mock surrender. "If that's your story." I shot him a look. I'd deal with him later.

I refocused my attention back on Nic, tears forming in my eyes. "I'm trying my hardest to pick up the pieces of my shattered life. But it's not easy. In fact, it's starting to feel like an impossible feat. My parents are gone. We may not have been all that close, but I loved knowing they were there if I needed," I sniffed sadly, refusing to let the tears fall free. "I don't have any real friends, human friends." I turned to Cody and Selene. "You two are the best friends I have ever had. Our friendship means more to me than you'll ever know."

Selene placed her hand on her heart, looking like she was about to cry herself. I wasn't even sure if vampires could cry. I'd have to add that to my mental list of things to ask them. Cody sat beside her, smiling wide. "You mean the world to us as well," he replied. I seriously loved those two.

"I left my job to come home, to come to Glenfall Heights. I don't even know who I am anymore," I said to Nic, barely above a whisper. "But the six of you welcomed me into your home. I feel closer to you than I ever have to any human before. Before, my parents were my only family. Now, you guys are. And I would really like to be a permanent part of this family. If you'll have me."

"Of course we will," Henri said, speaking up for the first time tonight. He was always thoughtful like that, not speaking until you had a chance to get everything off your chest. He was the first to get up and give me a hug. "You are already a part of this family, my dear. We would be honored if you would join us permanently."

"Thank you." I hugged him back, those darn tears forming back up. This time, I didn't care if they fell. And everyone saw.

One by one, the vampires came up and hugged me, welcoming me into their home, their lives, their family. I had never felt this level of acceptance before. Even Sergei was welcoming.

"I know I hated you at first," he began.

"You hated me?" I let out a mock gasp.

Sergei scrunched up his face. "Maybe not hated. I would say more of a strong dislike." He laughed. "But either way, welcome."

"I'm so excited to finally have a sister!" Selene almost knocked me to the ground with her strength again.

They left then, until it was just me and Nic standing alone in the common area. "You sure you know what you're doing?" He rubbed his hands up and down my arms. "This is what you truly want?"

"It is," I said, staring into his piercing blue eyes. "More than anything."

He didn't say anything for a couple minutes, making me afraid he was going to try to change my mind about everything. But then he said, "So I'll help you. I'll teach you everything there is to know about being a vampire, and I'll be there every step of the way through your transition."

My heart swelled. "Really?"

Nic lowered his forehead to mine. "Really. I promise, you won't ever have to be alone. And as for us," he pulled me closer, and my heart was pounding wildly in my chest, "I would love it if you were my girlfriend"

This day could not get any better. "I would love that, too," I answered. The world seemed to stop and fireworks exploded behind my eyelids as Nic kissed me, this time as my boyfriend, not just a guy I had a major crush on.

"Wow," I said breathlessly.

Nic let out a soft laugh. "I agree. Now, before we get into all the vampire stuff, I would like to take you on a proper date."

"I would love that."

Nic's lips parted in that sexy smile of his, and my breath hitched. "After, we can worry about teaching you all about being a vampire. Then, we'll pick a date and seal your doom." He laughed again, kissing me once more.

I couldn't wait to spend forever with this man.

ABOUT THE AUTHOR

J.M. Goodrich is a native of Michigan's beautiful upper peninsula. She loves spending time outdoors as much as she can with her family when she's not reading or writing. She has been published in several different anthologies and novels of her own. She has written stories of romance, fantasy, and horror. In addition to her love of writing, she has a passion for music, and an obsession with The Beatles.